Three Fantasies

JOHN COWPER POWYS

Three Fantasies

Afterword by Glen Cavaliero

CARCANET

First published in Great Britain 1985
by Carcanet Press Limited
208 Corn Exchange Buildings
Manchester M4 3BQ

The publishers acknowledge financial assistance from the
Arts Council of Great Britain

Powys, John Cowper
      Three fantasies.
      I. Title
      823'.912 [F]   PR6031.0867

      ISBN 0-85635-544-5

Typesetting by Paragon Photoset, Aylesbury
Printed in England by Short Run Press Ltd, Exeter

Contents

Topsy-Turvy

1

The Grey Armchair gazed across the little room at the Brown Armchair. They were in opposite corners; the grey one in the south corner and the brown one in the north corner of the room.

'Whirlwind and Whirlpool have left us quiet today,' said Mr Grey Armchair.

'I don't think it'll last long,' replied Mrs Brown Armchair, 'I seem to feel a certain motion of air coming in through the sides of the window.'

'I hope,' said Mr Grey Armchair, 'that they won't carry Topsy away again. I don't at all like seeing her whirled down our little square and carried over the wall into the green field. And it must be awful for Turvy. I saw him make a queer jerk when it happened last time just as he was going to shut the door.'

'He can't shut the door you know,' said Mrs Brown Armchair, 'because it won't shut after all those frantic jerks he once made to try and hold her back. It sort of closes, but it has never shut properly since then.'

'Poor Turvy!' sighed Mr Grey Armchair. 'How queer life in our room is! If it weren't for these visits of Whirlwind and Whirlpool we'd be fairly happy. Of course we never can be perfectly happy because of our own different views of things; but how quaint it is that we should all have souls that can move about and go away and return! Life in our room is indeed a strange thing. How it began we have no idea. How it will end we have no idea. Well, I suppose we must take it as it comes; but I can't help being sorry for Turvy when Topsy is in danger of being carried off, or at any rate when he thinks she is.'

'But don't you understand, you two silly old Armchairs,' said the Rocking-Chair that was under the picture of a Little Girls' Party which bore the name of Topsy and close to the door-handle which bore the name of Turvy, 'that it needs more experience of the Universe outside this little room of ours than either of you two have had, to understand these games of whirlwinds and whirlpools. I must have told you both thousands of times already that I, who was created in America out of materials purchased in New York City, am not in the least disturbed by the wild behaviour of these two lovers, one the soul of a pretty little picture and the other the soul of a jerky black door-handle. I was brought over here on a three-decked liner, so I know much more about the Great World outside this tiny little room than either of you do. And so, I warrant, you do also,' the Rocking-Chair went on, addressing the Carpet under all their feet which had come from Bokhara.

'I do! I do! I do!' cried the Carpet in a shrill little voice that sounded like the combined voices of a dozen baby mice. 'I know much more than those silly old Armchairs!'

It was at this moment that the great white Book-Case, with its six shelves full of books reaching from floor to ceiling, saw fit to intervene.

'What all you lively and quarrelsome folk seem to have quite forgotten,' the Book-Case announced, with its books from floor to ceiling supporting it, 'is that no one, in any civilized house in this country, can argue sensibly about pretty little pictures and competent door-handles, least of all a rocking-chair from New York City, without a deep and subtle knowledge of our Literature, especially of our Poetry, and of our famous translations of the Literature and Poetry of the ancient world. What do *you* say, Lemprière?' The great white Book-Case paused for a moment. 'What do you say, Aristophanes?' The top shelf shook as the Book-Case uttered the first name, and the second shelf shook as it uttered the second name. Then, descending to its third shelf, it uttered in a still more creaking tone: 'What do you say, Walt Whitman?' Then, descending to the fourth shelf, Landor was called upon. At the fifth shelf Lady Charlotte Guest was implored to say something; and finally from the lowest shelf of all, nearly touching the floor, an American History of all the Red Indian tribes was called upon to lift up its voice; which it did with a vengeance, making the whole room rattle.

During this noise little Topsy slipped back into her place above the Rocking-Chair and whispered to Turvy. 'Don't 'ee mind, darling! I didn't let Whirlwind carry me as far as it wanted to. It wanted to carry me to where Whirlpool was waiting to swallow me up. But I was too clever for the wicked old whoremonger. I pretended I wanted to take off some of my clothes before being swallowed up, but I said I was too shy to do it before anybody, so I begged to be allowed to go into that little wood called Bushes Home. But once there of course I skedaddled, and soon got into Wash Lane and over the wall into our Turnstile Corner.'

The Rocking-Chair, whose head nearly touched the tiny little picture of a children's Party, which was the bodily presence of Topsy, thought to itself, as it glanced sideways at the now complacent Door-Handle, who was contentedly keeping the cantankerous door closed: 'I must send my soul jockeying out, along with old Bottom-Step tomorrow, and visit the chimney-top, across Turnstile Corner where Whirlwind's nest is. I have a sort of idea that if I gave that whirligig this bit of red braid that's always coming off when I scratch my back I might be permitted to be present at the swallowing of Topsy by Whirlpool. Nothing, oh nothing, would give me greater satisfaction than to see Topsy go down Whirlpool's throat. Oh how angry that little chit of a starveling makes me feel when I see her playing at being pretty till that idiot of a Turn-Handle grows crazy as he dotes upon her. He's a decent little blackguard in himself but why can't he see what we all think of that little bitch?'

Sure enough when tomorrow came and it was about twelve o'clock midday and every soul in the little room upstairs was thinking of what it would do or pretend it was doing that afternoon, the soul of the Rocking-Chair clattered down the nine steps that led to Sideboard's parlour and Big Doll's and Little Doll's matrimonial bed.

'Ready to come out for a bit, Bottom-Step?' he said to the physically rather ponderous and mentally rather fuddyduddy gentleman in question.

'Well,' responded the Step thoughtfully, 'it might make a fellow feel more comfortable. All right, I'll come!'

The nest of these two vast Whirlabouts was at the top of a tall chimney at Turnstile Corner, just opposite the House with Nine Steps; and as the soul of Bottom-Step lumbered along behind the soul of Rocking-Chair they raised their eyes to this tall chimney. Yes! Both Whirlwind and Whirlpool were wallowing in their wayward thoughts. As they wriggled round each other in the watery nest they had made for themselves from the warped windpipe of a dying wizard, Mrs Whirlwind was saying to Mr Whirlpool, 'I feel sure, my dear, I'll be able to get you another chance of swallowing Topsy, and if Turvy's after her I'll have a go at him myself next time.'

'A nice day, you two!' said the Rocking-Chair, looking up.

'All well at home I hope?' said Mrs Whirlwind.

'Our old Turnstile Corner gets quite a deal of traffic, don't it, these days,' said Mr Whirlpool. 'How are you feeling, friend Bottom-Step?'

'Ask them,' whispered the soul of the Rocking-Chair to the soul of the Bottom-Step, 'at what time of day would they have the easiest fling at this little bitch Topsy.'

'In case,' said the dunder-headed Step, 'we happened to be taking Topsy for a walk, what would be the time of day that you'd like most to greet her?'

Mrs Whirlwind whispered something to Mr Whirlpool to which he responded with an ogrish grin. 'My husband says about six in the evening,' Mrs Whirlwind replied. 'But, of course,' she went on 'in our small world nothing goes always quite according to any arranged plan.'

'They're thinking,' whispered old Bottom-Step to his companion, 'that however well we time it there's always a chance that the wench may slip off as she did before.'

'Well, we'll bring her to greet you about six, just as you say,' concluded the Rocking-Chair.

In her parlour Mrs Sideboard Chest-of-Drawers was contemplating Big Doll and Little Doll as they talked together sitting on their bed, which Master Big Doll had just assisted Missy Little Doll in making very tidy. They had slept late, or rather Master Doll had slept till ten; and from ten to twelve till Rocking-Chair came ricketty-cricketty down the nine stairs, they had been talking together while they made their bed tidy. Big Doll had been telling Little Doll about their first night together in Mrs Sideboard Chest-of-Drawers' parlour, when he had explained to her that he never would ravish her because he didn't want to have the anxiety of their having children. 'When a Man-Doll as big as me,' he had told her, 'makes a Girl-Doll as little as you bear him children their tiny dolls become a great responsibility; whereas if Man-Doll and Girl-Doll just enjoy sleeping together without his ravishing her their life remains very happy and is free from all responsibility.'

'But perhaps,' Girl-Doll had replied, 'I should enjoy having a Baby Doll.' And at that reply, Man-Doll or Big-Doll remained silent while Girl-Doll or Little-Doll gave vent to several deep sighs.

Neither of them had realized that Mrs Sideboard Chest-of-Drawers was listening to their conversation as she reposed at a height half-way to the ceiling, while their bed was so low that it was near to the floor.

'Why was I so foolish,' thought Mrs Sideboard-Chest-of-Drawers to herself, 'as to adopt these kids when I came as a widow to this tiny house? Suppose they *had* decided to have a baby-doll what in heaven's name would I have done then? They wouldn't have known how to look after it and if it had died like my poor Tiny-Stool I should have perished with remorse.'

It was then that the great white Book-Case began addressing the King-Book in each of its six shelves:
'What do you say, Lemprière?
'What do you say, Aristophanes?
'What do you say, Walt Whitman?
'What do you say, Landor?
'What do you say, Lady Guest?
'What do you say, Red Indians?'

The speeches which all the six celebrities uttered were so vigorous that it was impossible for the Book-Case that contained them to disentangle one from another, till finally the war-whoops of the Red Indians drowned them all.

'I don't wonder,' said Mr Grey Armchair to Mrs Brown Armchair, 'that our gold-headed Poker in the grate here is getting agitated by all this fuss. I saw him stand up straight just now, didn't you, and begin to move, as if he would cross our fireplace from your side to mine.'

'No,' replied Mrs Brown Armchair, 'I was so deafened myself by all this hullabaloo that I didn't notice. Yes! by Saint Bartholomew you're right! He's clear across now and quite close to you! Look! Look! He's coming back to my side again! What's this you're up to? Don't you remember when I was little and Mother first got you I called you Excalibur because you made me think of King Arthur's sword? Mother reminded me of that story the last time she was here. I couldn't say Excalibur then, I called him Exy. Goodness! Where are you off to now, Exy?'

Both Armchairs jerked themselves a little forward, for to their astonishment they actually beheld Exy go thump, thump, thump, across the front of the great White Book-Case till it reached the space of about a yard between Book-Case and Door-Handle. Here it stopped and looked up at

Topsy, the Picture just about a couple of feet above its head. It must have trodden into some slit in the Carpet at this point, for it remained happily balanced where it was, staring up at the Picture.

'Isn't it queer, my dear, that we should all have souls in this little world of ours?' said Mrs Brown Armchair to Mr Grey Armchair. 'I know we have, not only because of that day when we both went downstairs to see what the Doll's Parlour on the ground-floor was like, but because the souls of Topsy the Picture and Turvy the Door-Handle have gone downstairs just now. I could feel their souls going with my soul, couldn't you with yours?'

Mr Grey Armchair nodded; and then he added, 'and not only their souls but the soul of your little Exy after them! His body may have got caught in the Carpet but his soul like that of old John Brown in the song goes marching on.'

'There are souls, I suppose,' said Mrs Brown Armchair, 'in every material thing in the whole world. And the whole world itself,' continued Mrs Brown Armchair, 'has probably got a soul of its enormous own, as conscious of itself as the souls of Earth, Sun, Moon, and Stars are conscious of themselves; and I certainly from the deepest depths of my soul believe that one day, perhaps thousands upon thousands of years away, all the different souls in the entirety of infinite space will approach one another and join together in a universal Celebration of Soul-Life.'

While these prophetic talks went on between the two Armchairs a very different sort of conversation was going on between Big Doll and Little Doll as they sat upon their bed, side by side. They spoke in so low a voice, though it wasn't exactly whispering, that neither Mr Grey Armchair nor Mrs Brown Armchair could hear what they were saying.

'Why have you been so sad lately, my precious little one?' said Big Doll to Little Doll. 'I've noticed this sadness in you ever since the night I decided not to rape you. Do you want to be raped, my darling?'

'Of course not,' replied Little Doll. 'I know it hurts terribly to be raped. The Kitchen-Cupboard over there told me that it made a girl cry till she screamed, it hurt so much. But he also told me, long before I decided that I would agree to sleep with you, that it was the only way to have a baby unless you went to a hospital to be artificially and scientifically raped; and nothing would induce me to do that. I am terrified of hospitals.'

'I don't want a child,' said Big Doll. 'You are the only child I'll ever love. Gee whizz! Why, my precious, we might have a child who was a reincarnation of some monstrous ancestor whose delight was to go about ravishing, killing and eating up little boys and girls, an ancestor like Blue-beard! Oh how awful that would be! Or we might have a child that was so seraphically pure-minded and angelic that it would regard with horror and loathing the very thought that its parents had been sexually attracted to each other and had gone through the process that produces children.'

'But I want a baby! Oh how I want a baby! Take me! Take me! O Bibabug! Bibabug! I do want a baby so!'

'Well you can't have one, Sillysuck, you just can't have one! I've got a horror of ravishing a little girl as sweet as you. I simply couldn't do it! It would be to me just what going to a hospital is to you. I refuse to do it. Surely we can be happy, loving each other and playing together, like we do, I with my what-do-you-call-it, and you with your what-do-you-call-it, both deliciously excited and tossing up and down, without going to this awful extreme of rending your virginity and making it bleed. I couldn't do it, I tell you. I've a horror of doing it.'

Sillysuck gave vent to a sigh so deep that it made her shiver from head to foot; and for a moment she thought in her heart, 'Suppose I let somebody else rape me, couldn't we both pretend that Bibabug had done it?' Big Doll heard this sigh; but if anybody had told him that Little Doll had actually for a moment considered the possibility of some-body else ravishing her he wouldn't have believed it. He would have even said to the Holy Ghost, if It had told him, 'You are a bloody liar!'

2

'Two days have gone by, haven't they, dearest, since we talked about that little girl Topsy who fooled us so?'

Thus spake Mrs Whirlwind to Mr Whirlpool as they sat in their nest in the top of the chimney on the house at the end of Turnstile Corner, just where the road curved round.

'Yes,' replied Mr Whirlpool, 'I've about given up all hope of swallowing that sweet morsel. Besides, after her narrow escape, isn't it extremely unlikely that she'll run such a risk again?'

'But you see, my dear,' said Mrs Whirlwind, 'that child Topsy has got a brother or a lover, or perhaps both-in-one, called Turvy who is a very spirited lad, so I have been told, and you know the confidence girls have in boys. Of course they are wrong to have such confidence, because, as anybody knows who has watched such a pair from our nest up here, it's the other way round; I mean it's the boy who ought to have confidence in the girl, for all girls are much wiser than all boys.'

'That's my old gal's mistake,' thought Mr Whirlpool as he settled down comfortably in their chimney-top nest, telling himself that when he was digesting that sweet little morsel of a tender maid it would be easier than usual to admit in words to his formidable wife that he was wrong and she was right.

'How are you two this cold evening?' came a voice from below. They both looked down and there was the soul of the New York Rocking-Chair beneath them, looking up with what seemed quite a friendly interest in his dark eyes.

'We are both very warm in our nest,' replied Mrs Whirlwind. 'We've got a splendid little Electric Heater up here that keeps us warm among our chimney-pots on the coldest nights. Won't you come up, good sir, and sit here with us for a bit? We know well who you are, for my husband and I have lived here since our marriage nearly half a century ago; and we know everybody round here.'

The soul of the Rocking-Chair muttered 'Thank you very much. I will indeed come.' Up he went and crouched down between them over their tiny Electric Heater. 'O this is delicious,' he gasped after an agreeable silence. 'May I ask where you two came from before you settled here?'

'We'll soon tell him all we know about that, won't we, hubby darling,' said Mrs Whirlwind, delighted to see the pleasure with which the soul of the Rocking-Chair from New York crouched down over the little Electric Heater in their nest at the top of the tall chimney. 'Well! My husband and I were born in Derbyshire, in a deep cave in the rocks above the River Dove. My husband was born in one cave and I was born in another. As children we used to wander quite far among the crevices and defiles of a particular district of the Pennines and we used to play at being grown-up married people with children of our own. There were the minnows and sticklebacks and newts and tadpoles that we found in the streams and kept in glass jars that we called aquariums.'

'Oh yes!' cried the soul of the Rocking-Chair, 'in the room on the ground floor of the house from which we come, the room nine steps down from the room which was my home, there is a kitchen cupboard full of precious things to eat. The cover of this cupboard used sometimes to fall off by its own weight, which was always a terrible distress to our Aunt Emma who looked after it. On the top of this cupboard there was a shelf up and down which Dick Turpin used to ride.' The soul of the Rocking-Chair was interrupted at this point by King Arthur's sword Excalibur, as the Brown Armchair and the Grey Armchair always allowed their golden-handled Poker to call himself. He had extricated himself from the hole in the Carpet where he had got stuck and had come thump, thump, thump, thump, down the nine steps from the room at the top.

'What are you doing up there?' cried the soul of the Poker to the soul of the Rocking-Chair.

'What the devil is that to you?' cried the soul of the Rocking-Chair in reply.

'They don't understand the Philosophy of Life, these things from the top room,' whispered Mrs Whirlwind to Mr Whirlpool. 'I think it comes from their living indoors like they do, instead of living out-of-doors as we do. You wait, hubby dear, till the souls of Topsy and Turvy come out of their house and walk to our end of Turnstile Corner! You shall have then, I swear to you, hubby darling, that sweet morsel of a girl to swallow, who escaped from us last time.'

'But may there not be,' said Turvy, 'some mysterious Destiny talk about something that was called "Another Dimension". Don't you think, my treasure, that this is what it is, Another Dimension? I hope none of those people from our upper room will follow us here and I hope still more that that Whirlwind couple won't come, or anybody from the ground floor room.'

'I don't believe they will!' gasped Topsy, her voice quivering with excitement, alarm, love, wonder and bewilderment. Moved by an irresistible impulse they both simultaneously turned round to look back. No! there was clearly no possibility of anyone following them for the vast rock-pillars of adamantine stone between which they had come had joined together as if some colossal superhuman hands had united them. Behind Topsy and Turvy there was nothing but an unbroken, stupendous Pamphylian precipice whose top was lost in mist.

3

They both hurried on, thankful beyond words that after the turmoil of their life they were alone and together, however much awed and thunderstruck by what they saw around them. Their path dissolved at once into what they saw. It was evidently only a kind of invitation from what they saw to enter into it and become part of it. What they saw around them was simply a mass of moving clouds, clouds that curved and curled and quivered and caracoled and circled and collapsed. The extraordinary thing about these clouds was that you could walk upon them! Yes! They had enough substance in them to hold a person up and enable a person not only to tread upon them but to lie down upon them. But Topsy and Turvy had not moved very far through this lively circus of encircling clouds before they looked at each other in bewildered astonishment. They were not alone! In every direction around them they beheld other human forms. The soul of Topsy, though her personality in their upstairs room had been a picture of little girls dancing, had taken care to clothe herself, when she went out with her lover, in appropriate and conventional girls' clothes. Turvy also, though he knew that his real self was the black handle of a creaky door, had seen to it that his soul wore the proper attire of a spirited young man going out into the world. He carried a hat and a stick, while Topsy carried a dainty brightly-coloured umbrella. It can be easily believed therefore that they were both staggered and utterly bewildered by what they saw around them. What they saw was an immense number of entirely naked men and women, people of all ages who were talking together in pairs or in groups or just quietly reclining upon clouds with an air of comfortable negligence. One of the pairs they were looking at came towards Topsy and Turvy as soon as they caught sight of them. This naked couple seemed about their own age. They approached them, smiling, and Topsy was rather shocked by the crudeness of Turvy's greeting.

'Who are you?' were his words.

'You have heard of us,' the naked girl answered with a bewitching smile, 'for our love for each other has been carried by poets and musicians all round the world.'

'Please tell us your names, oh beautiful ones,' said Topsy as persuasively as she could, thinking in her heart, 'I do pray Turvy won't be rude again.'

'How is it,' said the male partner of the pair, 'that you are both dressed? We are all taught in this paradise that it is bad manners and unkind to the clouds to confront them with dressed-up finery.'

'If one of you will tell me who you are, my friend, I will tell you who we are,' said Turvy.

'Don't talk like that, Turvy. Our names, Lady, our names, Sir, are Topsy and Turvy. I am a Picture from the upper room of our house, and my friend here is the Handle of the Door to our nine steps down. We will tell you all about ourselves and about the other things in our room upstairs, if you will be so kind as to tell us who you two are.'

Once more it was the beautiful naked girl who spoke, while her handsome companion glared at them offensively. 'We are Dido and Aeneas,' she said. 'I am the Queen of Carthage and this person comes from the Greek army which is besieging Troy. His mother is the Goddess Venus-Aphrodite and his father's name is Anchises. Come, Aeneas. The names of this pair are Topsy and Turvy. Their names, from what I have learnt of foreign languages, signify tumbling upside-down. They had no idea where they were when they entered cloud-land and still less when they asked us so roughly who we were. May I suggest,' Dido went on, still addressing her words to Topsy, for she clearly held the Amazonian conception of the sexes, namely that in wisdom and intelligence and value to the human race, women were infinitely more important than men, 'that we four sit down for a while on this cloud that is now between us, and then we can discuss all these things in quiet and peace. It is hard to think calmly and express our thoughts calmly when on the move. Our thoughts follow our motions. We notice a lot but we are too absorbed in what we see to philosophize about anything.'

Topsy glanced at Turvy whose face suggested no displeasure at Dido's idea; and they all four, Topsy and Turvy in their clothes and Dido and Aeneas stark naked, sat down upon the cloud, as they might have done upon a bench.

'What,' enquired Aeneas, 'would you say was your most difficult philosophical problem in connection with this human life which it is our destiny to live?'

This question was plainly addressed to Turvy, but Topsy replied. 'I can tell you my chief difficulty at once.'

'What is it? Do tell us,' said Dido.

'Well, I can't understand how our souls are so different from our bodies. My body is a little picture of a Children's Party. My friend's body is a Door-Handle. Now what would my soul look like if I were to see it in a Mirror? And what would the soul of my friend look like if we were to see it in a Mirror?'

'I think we can help you here,' replied Dido. 'Don't you think we can, Aeneas? You see, my dear friends, the soul of a thing is not quite like the soul of a person simply because a thing is different from a person. A thing is inanimate whereas a person is animate. But a thing *is* a thing, just as a person is a person; and as a person propels and ejects an image of himself or herself into the mind of every observer, so every inanimate thing projects an image of itself into the consciousness of everyone who observes it. These images or replicas or embodiments of the body — be it a rock or a beach or a tract of sand — possess all the consciousness that the body ever had. The human race and the whole race of animals tend to be jealous of the power of inanimates to rival them in consciousness. That is why dogs bark and cats miaow and bulls charge and mice nibble, at any statue or any picture or any image that strikes them as intruding upon their privileged position. Don't you see, my dear children, Dido went on, 'the fact that a Picture of Children at a Party, or a Door-Handle to a very tiresome Door, doesn't appear to possess any surviving self or that it is impossible for an outsider to imagine such a thing as a Picture thinking to itself "I am I" or a Door-Handle saying to itself "I shall never love anything as much as I love that Picture," doesn't affect the truth that such inanimates have surviving selves. There are a great many things in heaven and earth, as Hamlet says to Horatio, that we don't dream of; and prominent among such things is the Consciousness of Inanimates. Just think for a moment what human beings have come to feel about the Mountains of the Moon and the Signs of the Zodiac, the coming and going of Rainbows, and the movements of rain and hail and thunder and lightning. All these things strike us as possessing various sorts of mysterious purposes of their own and yet we have no more idea of the nature of these purposes than they have of the nature of our human or animal intentions.'

'But why, O wise Lady,' enquired Topsy, 'is the soul of a Picture able to move about like I can, and the soul of a Door-Handle able to move about like my friend here can? Are the souls of all inanimates able to move about independently of their bodies?'

'To answer that question as it deserves to be answered,' replied the Queen of Carthage, 'something more than the identity, as of a living self, belonging to the Inanimate of whom we speak, has to be considered. I refer to the impression made by this Inanimate upon human beings and upon animals. This impression remains in both the human and the animal mind and it is this impression which gives to the Inanimate's own awareness of itself as an entity a prerogative or procedure.'

'But your Majesty,' protested Topsy eagerly, 'doesn't the soul possessed by a human being or by an animal, whether it survives its body's death or not, have the appearance of the body which it represents?'

Dido and Aeneas exchanged a humorous smile. 'I am afraid I must confess,' said the former, 'that people and animals are sometimes so spirited that their spirits when they escape from their bodies, whether dead or alive, have the exact look of the bodies from which they issue forth. But I confess I cannot see any resemblance to a picture of a party of children in your face, my dear; and I certainly cannot see the faintest resemblance to a door-handle in your friend's manly countenance. So we have to assume, if we treat this important subject in a really philosophical way, that all souls emanating from inanimates are compelled by some inescapable Law of Nature to take the form, not of what they display of themselves to the world around them, but of men and women. If I were asked why this is so I should answer, as I am now going to answer you, though you haven't as yet faced me with such a question, like this. I should say that ever since the creative energy in Nature succeeded in giving birth to men and women it has made use of their forms as the best example of the shape any combination of matter should take when it feels within it the faintest consciousness of personal identity. This leads me, doesn't it, Aeneas?' and she looked at her husband with a certain hesitation, if not trepidation, 'to a further important point. Does the faintest existence of such conscious-ness imply of necessity the fact that it must be either a masculine consciousness or a feminine consciousness? I am inclined to think it does. Yes, I am inclined to think that from the largest human or animal creature to the smallest bird or fish or reptile or insect the difference between the two sexes definitely appears.'

'But do tell us, your Majesty,' pleaded Topsy, 'at what point does any fragment of matter have a right to claim that it contains the rudiments of consciousness?'

Dido smiled at Aeneas; but he didn't smile back. Perhaps this was one of those subjects upon which male and female creatures find difficulty in taking the same view. 'I think,' said the Queen of Carthage firmly, 'that this claim generally acquires its justification from the interest shown in the fragment of matter in question by beings already possessed of human or of animal consciousness or at least of a strong amount of it. You often see dogs sniffing and harrying such a fragment of half-conscious matter; and you know how little girls feel its existence in their dolls who to them are like their babies. Men with artistic instincts frequently become aware of an element of consciousness in the carvings, the statues, the pictures they admire, and sometimes even in the instruments they habitually use in the creation of these things, such as carving-tools and paintbrushes. And this is obviously especially true in the case of musical instruments such as flutes and harps, violins and guitars, harpsichords and pianos. You must remember my dears that there is a creative energy running through all the creatures of the universe. How absurd to deny, for instance, a vein of actual consciousness to all the carvings and pictures of great artists. The hand that created them has handed on its own inherent life to what it has created.'

'But please, your Majesty, do tell us how things like the little Picture which is I and the little Door-Handle which is Turvy can have a soul like the soul of a man or the soul of a woman, distinct and separate enough to go out and about quite independently of the body we leave behind and not associating itself with that body at all?'

'Your souls,' replied Dido, 'are, as I have just told you, shaped like the shape of a human being. When I look at you, Topsy, now, or at your friend, Turvy, now, I see a human form. Your two faces and the expression on each of them, have nothing to do with the picture you represent or the

door-handle your friend represents. Those two things, in
their disparate identities are simply the dwellings in which
you live. If I were to strike you it would not be in the least
like striking a picture nor if I were to strike your friend
would it be in the least like striking a door-handle.'

'But your Majesty,' protested Topsy, 'surely if I felt you
hitting me, the image of the Picture which is I would pass
through my mind? If I were, for instance, wandering
through a great forest far away from here, I might be
devoured by a lion. Would the fact that I had entirely
disappeared for ever have any effect on the picture whose
soul I am? Surely, your Majesty, if a thing has a soul and if
that soul is devoured by a lion far away from the thing
whose soul it is, the thing must feel it in some way, suffer
from it in some way? Are our souls and bodies, your
Majesty, so utterly different and so entirely independent of
each other, that the complete destruction of one of them has
no effect on the other? Look at it, your Majesty, the other
way round. Suppose now, at this moment while I am
talking to you, the Picture which is my body were smitten
to pieces by somebody entering the room where it hangs on
the wall, would I be unaffected by it and just walk on where
I was walking, in complete indifference? And what, your
Majesty should I feel when I came back to the room and
found my body stricken to bits and lying in little pieces on
the floor?'

The Queen of Carthage hesitated for two or three long
moments. Then she said quietly, 'I am afraid, my dear
child, that, just as you so tragically hint, there *does* exist this
fatal difference between our bodies and our souls. The truth
is, little lady, that this life of ours, wherever we are, is no
joke. Of course that is exactly what lots of satirical writers
have always said it was. But I disagree, and so does Aeneas
— don't you Aeneas? — we both feel, as I expect not only
you but your friend Turvy does too, that we have to make a
definite effort of the mind to be happy. Let us lie back on
Fate and let us be ready to accept Chance; but, while our

soul remains in its body, both the soul within and the body without must work together so that both can be happy. Oh how afraid I was that Aeneas would forget me! Wasn't I, Aeneas? And you see, my sweet child, he didn't forget me; he came back to me and I've been happy with him ever since. It is the same with our body and our soul. But if our soul doesn't come home — for that is what our body is to our soul, it's its home — and if as you suggest, our home were broken into bits, as any house might be by an earthquake or a whirlwind, well, what is there left us to do but to find another home? Yes, to hunt about till we find some body that is as lost as we are. Then we shall become a lost soul in a lost body. But not for long! The new partners will coalesce and there will soon be the same sort of love between them as there was of old between the former pair. Am I not right, Aeneas? Though you and I have been spared this weird experience we would be able to adjust ourselves to it, wouldn't we, you to another woman and I to another man?'

It was then that Topsy and Turvy suffered a shock.

'No!' cried Aeneas, in a thundering voice, 'No! Never would I mate with anyone else. I couldn't! I wouldn't! The mere thought of it makes me feel murderous! Come along, Dido! You've talked to these children long enough! I'll tell them one thing before you go off with me; and *that* is, they'd better cast off their silly clothes and be as stark naked in this Dimension of the Truth as the rest of us are!' Thus speaking he seized Dido by the wrist and dragged her away.

Topsy and Turvy were both so disturbed by the violent behaviour of Aeneas that they remained seated on the cloud where the Queen of Carthage had been talking to them and did not dare to move. The idea of taking off their clothes was equally repugnant to both of them though they did whisper to each other that they felt rather uncomfortably warm and Turvy told Topsy that he could see drops of perspiration on her forehead. They were still in the same position upon the same cloud when they saw two very friendly-looking persons, a man and a woman, coming to speak to them. Topsy and Turvy got up politely to welcome this couple and the man said at once, 'Sit you down, my dears, and let's talk of the world from which we've come. This is my friend and Theatre-Manager, Henry Irving.

'Oh Sir: Oh Lady!' our friends cried simultaneously, making room for them both by their sides. 'We've both longed to go to London to see you, but we've lived a very limited life and have never had the chance,' said Turvy.

'You'd be surprised if we told you what we are at home,' said Topsy. 'But I expect,' she went on, 'famous people like you two have often had in your audiences, perhaps without knowing it, people with quite as simple a background as what we two have come from.'

'It's not what life has made of us,' said Henry Irving, 'but what we have made of life that counts. Miss Terry and I have seen many queer people in our time, haven't we, Ellen? And many famous people too, and I daresay when we learn your names we shall find that you two are well known in the great world.'

'Alas! no, great sir,' cried Topsy rather pathetically, 'we've never had any chance, either of us. My friend Turvy would have made a very good actor, I am sure of that, if you had taken him into your Company.'

'And you a good actress, my dear,' said Ellen Terry tenderly. 'I can see you've got the most important quality for good acting.'

'What's that, Lady?' enquired Turvy eagerly.

'Well, my dear man,' said Miss Terry 'I think I might call it bravery! I mean the spirit to plunge into the part you've been given and not let shyness or nervousness or any sort of self-conscious fear hold you back from asserting yourself and expressing the feelings of the part you have to play.'

'From what kind of background,' enquired Henry Irving, 'did you two come?'

'Oh I'll tell you at once!' cried Turvy. 'When at home I am the Handle of a very creaky Door, a door that's hard to shut. And Topsy here is a Picture painted by a little girl of a children's dance.'

Henry Irving looked excitedly at Ellen Terry. 'Wasn't I telling you only yesterday, my dear, that if the old pieces of furniture in my Aunt Brodribb's drawing-room could turn into actors and actresses the suppressed life of half a century would become vocal? These youngsters are perfectly right. There are chairs and tables and chimney-pieces and foot-stools in old-fashioned rooms that could make us all laugh and cry if they could only speak.'

Both Topsy and Turvy were delighted at Henry Irving's words; and Turvy asked, 'Do tell us, Master, why it is that the souls of things are so different from the bodies of things? Why is it that the souls of such a variety of things as Pictures, Handles, Cupboards, Fenders, Coal-scuttles, Pokers, Tongs, Carpets, Rugs, Chairs and Tables as well as Rocks and Stones and Chimney-tops should all have the same sort of soul, namely a soul with the image of a Man, which according to the Bible is the image of God?'

'I think,' said Irving gravely, 'that you've hit on the right track. Was not the first living creature in the Universe an amoeba in the salt sea, that "microscopic animalcule" as the Fowlers say in their Oxford Dictionary, which splits itself into two halves, each half becoming a new amoeba and thus perpetuating the amoebic race? And does not that remind us how in order to have children the man must break the virginity of the woman or else their race will die out? Only through secretive violence of this kind does humanity progress.'

Topsy was beginning to utter something that Turvy feared might offend Henry Irving and Ellen Terry, when suddenly the great Actor and his Actress were completely upset by the appearance of a big black horse with a man on its back who, like the rest of the men and women in this weird Dimension, was stark naked, galloping towards them at top speed.

'Come Ellen, come quick!' cried the great Actor, for

whom evidently black horses driven out of all control by
something or somebody was an untheatrical and unseemly
thing. 'We must clear out of this!' And off they both ran,
seeking refuge behind a large group of naked people who
were listening to some sort of preacher. Our two friends
stood up; and as they did so an airy cloud, full, Turvy
thought, of tiny snow-white birds, plucked at their clothes
and carried off everything they wore, leaving them as naked
as all the other human beings in this strange Dimension of
Life's Truth. As for a quick moment they looked at each
other Turvy was absolutely amazed at the beauty of Topsy
— he had never dreamed she was as lovely as this. Then they
both made a feeble attempt to stop the Black Horse. To
their surprise however a spirited girl and an athletic man
and a queer old parson or priest of some sort, who were
talking together, rushed forward to help them and soon
brought the black steed, who turned out to be a mare, to a
complete stop, while her rider slipped from her back to the
ground.

   'What's this?' he cried indignantly. 'Don't any of you
bounders and molly-coddle shirkers know who I am? I am
Dick Turpin and by Jerubbabel I'll tie the lot of ye to Squire
Hazelbury's drive gate and use my whip on ye instead of on
poor old Black Bess who'll probably die of jitterbugs before
my next birthday.'

   It was then to Topsy's and Turvy's astonishment that the
gay rollicking leader of the group who had helped them to
stop the mare cried, 'Who cares who you are, you bouncing
blob of cat's spue! Who cares from what pigstye shittery
you come, you bumbledy-blummery flap-pot!'

   'Everybody knows who I am,' cried the rider, who had
gathered the reins tightly in one hand while he brandished
his whip in the other at those who had blocked his path. 'I
am Dick Turpin and my mare Black Bess is known to all the
world. How dare you meddle with me and her you bam-
bery-bumbery set of stinkhards?'

   The leader of the gang who had stopped Dick Turpin and

Black Bess now came forward. The two men began be-labouring each other with filthy abuse, while every now and then the sprightly young girl who clearly was the darling of these newcomers, patted Black Bess on her shoulder so tenderly that the mare turned her head towards her, heedless of her master's reins or whip. 'Don't make too much fuss, Robin Hood,' said his priestly-looking companion. 'Leave the mare to Maid Marion. She's begun to win the beast's favour already. In a little while we'll be having them both at our command and then we can decide what to do with them.'

'You shut up, Friar Tuck,' protested Robin Hood. 'Keep your sermon till we've got the fellow under control — then we'll show him where he's got off.'

'But don't you see, Robin Hood, old boy, if we don't get the Mare quiet and get his whip out of the fellow's hand, we shall never have them as we want them. Let her stay quietly with us, Master Turpin, and you yourself had better stay quietly with us too. You must understand that you have been led on by your mania for riding at top speed and overtaking coaches full of quiet folk and robbing them of every penny they've got, into the ridiculous illusion that you are the only highwayman in Britain. Let me get it now once for all into your stupid skull that you are anything but that. By far the most successful highway freebooters this country knows are we who have now brought you to book. I expect you are wondering' — and it certainly did look as if Dick Turpin, as he stood with one hand on Black Bess's rump and the other, from the fingers of which the whip was trailing to the ground, on the back of her saddle, was in a maze of bewilderment — 'why we don't knock you on the head at once since we are two to one. Well, I will tell you why we don't. We don't knock you on the head for good and all because it has crossed our minds that with your aid and the aid of your mare, if we joined forces, we might grow as rich as any of these damned Squire Hazelburys, whose gates we're always passing.'

4

What Robin Hood and Friar Tuck and Maid Marion must
have had in their minds from the start, when they first
encountered Dick Turpin galloping up on Black Bess, was
now evidently fulfilled. They *were* going to work in unison
and with the full intent of becoming the most successful and
the richest bandits ever yet known in our island.

But Topsy and Turvy had ceased to care how few or how
many composed the gang. It was surely impossible, both
our friends thought, for this Confederation of Bandits to
play their part in a world that had no highways at all and
where everybody was naked in a rock-a-bye ocean of
drifting clouds. 'I suppose,' said Topsy to Turvy, 'that they
are all ghosts and that the whole thing is really a sort of
catch-me-out charade among the souls of the dead.'

'I certainly can't imagine coaches passing down broad
roads down here,' replied Turvy, 'and yet that mare, Black
Bess, is clearly not a ghost.'

'Let's go away from here,' said Topsy to Turvy, 'I'm
tired of the company of these robbers. Let's try to find some
nicer companions.'

'Where the devil shall we go?' said Turvy to Topsy. 'In
this damned place they'll all be a funny lot.'

'Let's try any way,' said Topsy to Turvy. 'You never
know down here, or up here, or round about here, what
you may find.'

So they wandered off among the rolling clouds and the

drifting naked people. Quite a long way they went. But at last they saw, not far off, two forms whose appearance attracted both of them quite a lot. One was a bearded man and the other was a youth who was clean-shaven except for a faintly outlined slight moustache. These two were talking together excitedly while the cloud beneath them acted as if it wanted to throw them off.

'Forgive my impertinence,' said Topsy, addressing them both in her most charming manner, 'but do you mind our asking who you are? We have come from a house in North Wales. I am Topsy and my friend is Turvy; and the only things we're afraid of are Whirlwinds and Whirlpools.'

'This cloud here is called Manhattan,' said the bearded man buoyantly, 'but my friend here keeps talking about beautiful girls he has lost and about the places where they're buried. I mustn't make you jealous, sir, by praising your lady but I don't believe I've ever seen in all my life on earth a more beautiful girl than you are.' And in place of bowing or making any other conventional gesture of respect, he patted Topsy on the head as if she had been his grandchild. Topsy was delighted at such treatment which she greatly preferred to more fashionable signs of admiration, and she smiled gaily at the bearded man.

'Oh Walt, Walt!' expostulated his friend, 'but you must remember that we have all got to keep up the ancient worship of beauty that has come down to us from an antiquity more ancient and more sacred than any of us know. The worship of beauty is the secret underlying inspiration of all life. It goes much deeper, it has lasted much longer than any of these exacting religions whose adherents call them old and sacred. I tell you, Walt old boy, that Baltimore in Maryland is worth a thousand of your damned Manhattan Islands. I know what I am talking about; for my unsurpassably beautiful girl has a still more beautiful Mother and I worship them both equally. I am not saying that this arrogant Mr Allan who picked me up as a kid and patronized me so condescendingly isn't a noble or gracious personage. What I am saying is that my beautiful girl and her still more beautiful mother are the symbols and living embodiments of a tradition far older than Christianity and far older than those Olympian gods and their pet boys and girls in Rome on the Tiber or London on the Thames or Paris on the Seine or Frankfurt on the Main. In the ancient rocks and caves of every hillside in Europe and Asia there are images of the worship of beauty that go back to a day before human history as it is recorded in written books began. Yes! go back to ages when pictures of men and women and boys and girls and beasts of the field and birds of the air recorded a worship of beauty older than all that has been written in the words of any known language or in the rhythms of any known verse. I tell you, Walt Whitman, it's all very well for you to comfort the wounded in hospitals and sit down with all the magic of your splendid manhood by sick men's beds and gather their spirits up in the guise of a new Messiah, but long before God deserted Jesus on the Cross, and long before Mohammed wrote the Koran, and long before Gautama Buddha preached to the wise the wisdom that sinks in peace into everlasting silence, the mystery of Beauty dominated human life and inspired the minds of men, women, and children as it has done ever since the amoeba in the depths of the sea split itself in two. What you don't or won't understand, you excitable old Walt, is the existence of beauty round and about us in the simplest and most ordinary things. There is beauty in the way a cupboard stands out from the wall against which it is fixed, making an extremely impressive angle. There is beauty in the way a mantelpiece supported at both ends by pillars descending to the floor, stretches across the fireplace. There is beauty about the angle between the ceiling and the walls in every room we live in, not to mention the terrifying secretiveness of each particular corner, suggestive of desperation and escape from hell. Nor is there anything more redolent of dramatic experience than a carpet, or still more than a rug, especially one from Persia or Assyria. And what armchair is there in any apartment in the world, whether with a footstool of gold from Babylon or a footstool of ebony from Ethiopia, that does not suggest between its welcoming arms a seat for a Conqueror of Mesopotamia or a cushion for the thighs of a Cytherean Aphrodite?'

Before Walt Whitman could answer this oration on the antiquity and divinity of Beauty by Edgar Allan Poe both Topsy and Turvy broke in, 'I should like to say that in these ordinary things, like armchairs and rugs, which you are praising for their beauty there is something else much more important than beauty.'

'She means *use*, don't you Topsy?' cried Turvy excitedly. '*Use* is the important thing. I tell you it wasn't their beauty at all, whatever footstools or cushions they had, that made those armchairs you are talking about so nice. It was their *use*! I can well imagine — can't you Topsy? — an armchair with a very ugly cover that would be just as useful as any other! Surely you two gentlemen see what we mean?'

Walt Whitman gave his beard a little push forward with one of his hands and allowed his head to sway a little from side to side, as if he were following the music of some unseen instrument.

'To tell you the truth, my dear children,' he said, 'and I include you too, Edgar Poe, in what I am saying, the real secret of our lives is neither the use of things nor the beauty of things; nor is it the things themselves, even if you are talking about the scenery for a great picture with forest and fountains and mountains and the distant sea. The secret of our lives is in us, I tell you, yes! in our hearts and minds and feelings! The key to life lies in two simple words: I LIVE. It is our I, my dear children, the real deep mysterious unknowable *self* in each one of us, the self in men, women, and children, the self in animals, vegetables and minerals, the self in birds and reptiles and fishes, the self in every insect in the world, as well as the self in the sun, in the moon, in every star! I tell you, Edgar Poe, I tell you, you darling pair of lovers, the whole secret of life lies in ourselves; nowhere,

nowhere, nowhere, nowhere else! These clever, inventive, scientific technicians have all manner of wonderful and miraculous secrets. But one secret they have *not* got; they have *not* got the secret of life. They can go on telling you that the beginning of life is the element from which life springs. They can tell you that it's in fire, in water, in earth, in air, in space. But they are wrong. In all elements there is Life. But Life is not the element from which it comes. *Life is consciousness.* Without consciousness there is no Life: there is only the empty house waiting for Life to fill it. The greatest oceans, the greatest mountains, are only the dwellings that Life must enter by way of consciousness. If there were not consciousness within them they would cease to exist. Yes! They would be totally unreal. They would be only *visions*, the visions of some living thing that has consciousness. You hear people talk, my children, about Mind and Matter. I tell you there are no such things! Mind and Matter are just dictionary words invented by the consciousnesses who construct dictionaries. No amount of mind could make a particle of matter, no amount of matter could make a particle of mind. They need a living Self.'

Whether it was the projected beard of Walt Whitman or the strange wild light in the eyes of Edgar Poe, there was something about the dead silence that followed the former's dissertations upon Self and Selves that caused a queer simultaneous terror to seize upon both Topsy and Turvy. And without a word to either of their famous interlocutors they just jumped to their feet and ran at top speed towards an especially dense cloud which could be seen heaving and toppling about a mile away. It didn't take them long to reach it for they were both swift on their feet; but they were surprised when they reached the cloud to find that there was a rather startling absence of naked persons in that cloud's immediate vicinity. But they quickly realized the reason. There were two crowned heads seated together at the cloud's base, with their backs against it, and as it swayed backwards and forwards their argument, which was clearly a genuine dispute, got more and more vehement.

'What you keep forgetting, you confounded Saxon,' King Canute was shouting when they came on the scene, 'is that we are both ghosts now, and that when we lived we never confronted each other in battle. It was our sons and our sons' sons who fought with each other! No, I'm not saying', the Danish monarch went on, 'that you, Alfred the Great of Wessex, weren't a good sovereign to your people; for you were. That was why I sent most of my fleet and most of my soldiers back to their homeland. I wanted to be as good a monarch of this country, of both our two countries together, as everybody told me you had been in your time. What you don't seem to realize is that there's a close link of racial blood, yes of northern blood, between our two lands; so that it became almost as easy for me to surround myself with English lords and chiefs as with rulers and captains of my own blood.'

Canute was silent for a moment. But his richly resounding voice was still echoing round them when King Alfred's deep, firm, vigorous Saxon voice made itself audible like the sound of a powerful blacksmith's hammer striking an iron anvil.

'You may say what you like; your words are but belching wind to the ears of any honest and faithful Englishman. Nearer related no doubt we are than either of us to these damned Normans and Flemings and Franks from the other side of our English Channel. But though we are nearer to each other than any of these scurvy Frenchmen, that doesn't give you the right to talk as if we lost one of our grandest opportunities to be the most dominant country between Rome and Iceland by not allowing ourselves to be permanently ruled by Danes. Shall I tell you, you boastful and overbearing ghost of what could not be, cannot be, and will not be, what is the best embodiment of the voice of destiny uttering the true prediction and predestination? I tell you, you arrogant claimer of that to which you know you have no right, it is the universal voice of young students of our history in the schools of our land; and it is from there that the rumoured legendary voices reach us still murmuring of how Canute warned his courtiers that he could not command the sequence of the tides upon the coast and the significant and natural story in all its simple homeliness of Alfred King of England and those cakes of his.'

5

'Let's get away from here, my precious,' whispered Turvy to Topsy. 'I don't like watching those two naked men with crowns on their bare heads arguing with each other. I'm all for Alfred, if we had to choose, and I warrant you are too, but we don't have to choose. Let's skedaddle! As Ellen Terry said she did when George Bernard Shaw went up to bully Henry Irving.'

Topsy nodded and gave him her hand and off they ran. Once more among the crowd of ordinary naked ones, mingled with extraordinary naked ones, they alternated between running and strolling and between dead silences and lively chatter. At last they stopped dead. 'Who on earth are those two?' whispered Topsy to Turvy. 'Good Lord! What a pair!' murmured Turvy. 'Let's go and see!' They soon reached the couple who had attracted them; and Topsy whispered excitedly to Turvy at once: 'It's Samson and Delilah! Look at them! Listen to them!' They certainly never in their lives had seen a quarrel between husband and wife equal to what they saw now.

'What I would like best to see,' the wife was saying, 'would be the Chief Executioner of the Philistines standing upon your body, naked as it is now, and very carefully and slowly cutting out all your principal organs one by one and arranging them separately on a silver plate at your side. When it comes to your testicles, or knackers, or balls, as my little brother told me they called them at school, I should like to see him put them on the plate with the rest but on the opposite side, not close together. They are the things I have suffered from: and I want to see *them* suffer in their turn. Oh yes! And your villainous penis, or prick, as my little brother said they called it at school, that I would love to see *cut off* and laid in the centre of the plate with its head propped up on a little pebble so that it would point upwards into the clouds, the winds, while its voice would cry pitifully "I'm dissolving! I'm going! I'll soon be lost forever!" '

'Can't you hold your whoresome tongue for one single second?' groaned the voice of Samson. 'If I weren't brought up in the courts of the Lord I would teach you how to talk to me like this!'

Topsy and Turvy had had enough by this time of Delilah's talk and of Samson's terrific muscles, which were quivering with wrath. So they just took to their heels and fled.

They were pulled up with interest and with amazement by an exciting discussion, amounting to an indignant dispute at moments, between a group of famous writers: namely, Rudyard Kipling, Rider Haggard, Bulwer Lytton, and Harrison Ainsworth.

'Who are you two? And where do you come from?' cried Bulwer Lytton.

Topsy, catching the eye of Harrison Ainsworth, after making a dainty little curtsey, answered, 'We come from North Wales and we live in the most beautiful county in all the British Isles.'

'What may that be?' enquired Rudyard Kipling.

'Merioneth,' answered Turvy, loudly and boldly. 'On one coast we have a shore with the most transparent and lovely pebbles to be found anywhere except at Chesil Beach in Dorset; and on our opposite coast we have the most beautiful shells to be found on any shore in England or Scotland or Ireland!'

'Well, my dears,' said Rudyard Kipling, 'I wonder if either of you have ever been to Brighton?'

'Or to Eastbourne?' cried Rider Haggard. 'Beachy Head has the grandest sea view on the whole of our English coast.'

'Of course,' said Bulwer Lytton, 'not one of the seaside places in England or Scotland can compare for a moment with Naples or with what you see at Pompeii or in Sicily or in Capri. You have no volcanic mountains and no seashores or sea-islands or sea-palaces anywhere to compare with what the gondolas in Venice take you to see.'

'Shut your mouth, Bulwer!' cried Kipling. 'If this couple could see Brighton beach they would see something as good as any of your damned volcanic mountains!'

'What interests us, gentlemen,' said Turvy, once more speaking out louder and bolder than Topsy quite liked to hear him speak, 'is a matter to which all of you four great writers have referred as you told your thrilling and absorbing romances, but a matter all the same that the impetuosity of your astonishing inspirations prevented you from developing or enlarging upon. I am speaking of the events in my girl-friend's life and mine that brought us into this startling and awe-inspiring Dimension where all we naked mortals are encountering the Truth of Life. These events, gentlemen, and please understand that we have both read and absorbed into our bodies and souls the great romantic novels of each one of you four mighty geniuses, are simply the natural causes that led to our loving each other and setting out together on a life of adventure. You see, oh great and famous gentlemen, we both come from the upper room of a tiny half-house which has only two storeys separated by a little staircase of nine steps, one the ground floor and one the first upper floor beyond which is nothing, no attic roof at all. In our tiny upper room, oh great and famous gentlemen, there is only a fireplace with a mantelpiece above it and a poker beside it, two armchairs, and a tall book-case from floor to ceiling. The body of my girl-friend is a Picture by a little girl of fourteen of a child's party and my own body is a black Handle to a very creaky door close to this Picture. We ran down the stairs together, holding hands, and then had to rush as fast as our legs could carry us round the curve of a road called Turnstile where Mrs Whirlwind and Mr Whirlpool tried to catch us because Mr Whirlpool wanted to swallow my girl Topsy. It was then that we were suddenly attracted to a little by-path that precipitated us to our astonishment into this Dimension of naked reality where we are now talking to you. Do please tell us, oh Mighty Four, in what way this Dimension of the Naked Truth of Life differs from the place, wherever it may be, to which the ghosts of all who die upon our earth depart when their bodies are dead. Do they go straight to heaven or hell or to some intermediate purgatory?'

'If we only had a wise lady among us,' replied Harrison Ainsworth, 'I warrant we could answer your question at once.'

'But she'd have to be a little more than just wise,' replied Rider Haggard. 'She'd have to have the sort of intuition in her that the greatest of witches have.'

'She'd have to have the wisdom of a terrific king-wizard,' cried Bulwer Lytton eagerly. 'There are women like that, you know: like Saint Anne the Mother of Mary.'

'What are you saying!' growled Rudyard Kipling. 'You talk like one of those Blacks who are the chief burden of us intelligent Whites.'

'All I can say,' burst out Bulwer Lytton, 'is that I wish the whole of Africa were inhabited by Blacks and ruled by Blacks and that the only business we sensible Britishers and sensible Americans had was to see to it that the Yellow Peril was nipped in the bud!'

'They're all too clever for us,' whispered Topsy to Turvy, 'let's make a bolt for it and be off!'

6

What stopped their run and pulled them up short were the terrific gestures of an enormous Negro. The group this Negro was addressing was well known to both our friends in one sense, that is to say because each of the faces composing the group was a face that had been pictured again and again in children's illustrated histories. This will be well understood when it is explained that one face was that of a very early King of Rome whose name was Numa, another the face of a delicate Nymph or exquisitely pretty young girl who lived in a cave in that same early Rome and was visited every day by King Numa, and who taught him by degrees the exact steps to take in order to conquer the world and establish over it the Roman Empire.

The excited talk in this group of recognizable persons was emphasized by the fact that one was clearly an Anglican Bishop and one a particularly seductive and appealing little London Street-Walker. Then there was the excited Negro who kept shouting, 'I am only a Black! I am only a Black! But the day will come when someone like me will rule the whole of Africa from south to north and from east to west! Africa, I tell you, you crazy world of every race that exists, will one day be entirely governed, yes, from north to south and from east to west, by black men like me! So you'd better prepare for that, you other races of the world, if you wish to survive!'

As a fine contrast to this excited black man there now

came from this group an elaborately tuneful voice, a voice so rich and melodious that it seemed to be saying in a rhythmic prose almost worthy of rivalling the *Urn-Burial* of Sir Thomas Browne, 'I am only Thomas De Quincey but I hold the opinion that what the enemies of rich prose call a mere string of purple passages is what is needed to keep the music of the English language alive. And if you ask me,' De Quincey went on, 'what living human being there is who in her own delicate, exquisite, and unselfish personality offers a parallel to the exquisite harmony of what vulgar-minded people despise as a string of purple passages, I shall point till the end of my days to a certain little London prostitute or street-walker or whore by whose noble unselfishness my own sick and wretched life was restored to me.'

'I'm not worthy! I'm not worthy! I'm not worthy of what he says!' came in a young girl's voice from a slender little girl at his side.

'You did, you did, you did, my precious little Ann,' repeated De Quincey, 'you did. You saved my life and all of my work that was worth saving for posterity by what you did for me! I won't let you deny it! I won't let you! I won't let you!'

'I am mighty glad,' broke in the deep resonant voice of King Numa of Rome. 'Yes! I am mighty glad to learn that in Londinium on the River Tamesis in a far-away island there are lovely ladies who have the power to do for a man what no other man can do and what no wife however queenly can do, but what my Egeria, my beautiful nymph in her secret cavern in this rocky gorge can do, is doing, and will do while we both live, for a thick-skulled, crinky-cranky, muddle-headed old ruler like me. I'll show you, yes, by Jupiter and his father Chronos, I'll show you what a stupid old monarch becomes when he has a Nymph like Egeria to help him! You wait and see, you warrior races! With Egeria to help me I will conquer the whole world for Rome.'

'Would it be right to ask your gracious Majesty if with my little friend Ann I might have an interview with Egeria, the Nymph in Antro? I would not presume to ask for your presence there, oh great King, or for any interview with you personally; but I would regard it as the greatest moment of my whole life if you would let me take my little Ann and introduce her to Egeria in her rocky cave.'

'Yes, you certainly shall take your lovely little Nymph to visit *my* lovely little Nymph,' said King Numa graciously, 'and I can only wish that in your life, my good sir, the influence of your Nymph upon you will be as momentous and memorable as mine I feel is going to prove upon me.'

At this moment, in a gilded bag which King Numa was carrying in his hand, a clock began to strike. The monarch held it up to his right ear and listened intently to what the clock said. Topsy and Turvy listened too and so more intently still did De Quincey. It must have been a very powerful clock and a very musical clock; for even the fierce Negro who had been muttering to himself all this while, as he stared at Topsy and Turvy, listened spellbound along with the rest of them. 'One, two, three, four, five, six, seven, eight, *nine*' struck the clock.

'You all know, don't you, what clock is striking and where?' said the King of Rome. 'It is Big Ben in London and they tell me everywhere in Britain that it's unlucky for you if you hear it beginning to strike, not to listen to the end, counting the strokes.'

The fierce Negro sprang to his feet from where he had been crouching and muttering. 'I say, may hell and damnation seize these accursed English and their bloody Big Ben! I tell you, King of Rome, I tell you, you pretty little travellers from England, the men who are going to rule Africa are Africans! Yes! None others! Not your blasted Red Indians of America, not your far more blasted Dutchmen in South Africa with their fucking apartheid or "keep the races separate!" We'll "apartheid" you, you bloody Dutchmen, we'll turn you into good meat for honest niggers, you blasted Boers! I tell you all, whether you are brutal Dutchmen or self-conceited, showing-off, snobbish English, there'll come a time and pretty soon it'll come too, when the folk who rule Africa will be the folk to whom Africa gave birth. And *they* weren't nurtured in England, or in America, or in Australia, or New Zealand either! Africa gave them birth — Africa was their mother. And I tell every single one of you who will beget and conceive children on the soil of Africa, your descendants will be swept off the earth by Africa's real sons and daughters. Don't make any mistake, oh you mumbling and bumbling false prophets of apartheid! Africa herself speaks through me who alone among you all out here, big kings and dainty whores and wily travellers, am her true and faithful child. Yes, I tell you, Africa speaks through me; and one day the descendants of all you bastard interlopers will find it out to your cost!'

The slim little girl who was resting her hand on the arm of Thomas De Quincey suddenly came up to Topsy. Her clothes, like Topsy's, had already fallen off and she and Topsy looked like a pair of sweet little sisters together. 'I am very fond of my man here,' whispered little Ann to Topsy, 'as I bet you're very fond of yours, but it's a comfort to me, a comfort I am sure you can well understand, to be able to talk to a girl of my own age in this funny land of nakedness. I was able to be a saving help to my friend as I am sure you must have been to yours; but I never expected to find myself with him in a place like this. My friend Mr De Quincey calls this place "the Fourth Dimension". What on earth he means by that I don't know. Do tell me what your man calls it.'

'Well, my dear Ann, I don't believe' — here Topsy hesitated a little — 'that my man is as learned as yours. But I expect the household we come from is less learned than either of you. Your Mr De Quincey, my dear Ann, as I can tell, is a scholar who knows Latin and Greek, neither Turvy nor I know a word of those languages. I expect it'll be hard for you to believe, but I'd better tell you at once that what you would call our *bodies* before we became naked ghosts, if we *are* ghosts here, or at any rate naked males and females or naked masculines and feminines, were nothing but pieces of furniture in a room in a house. These pieces of furniture had the sort of consciousness in them that human beings have. But they were not — I mean we were not — human beings at all. We were chairs and tables and book-cases and mantel-pieces and pokers and tongs and carpets and antimacassars and pictures and writing-desks and footstools and all sorts of china ornaments and all sorts of lesson-books and picture-books and story-books. Some of us were lamps and candles and match boxes and a lot of us were toys and dolls' houses, and even bricks to build fairy castles with.'

'You see, my dear child,' broke in Turvy, for he felt a bit jealous of Topsy's having the whole pulpit just now, 'people have not realized the amount of livingness that comes to exist in every piece of furniture that has been for many years the background of human lives. When from babyhood up to seventeen or eighteen or twenty a person, whether male or female, has lived with certain chairs and tables and pictures and rugs and carpets and cupboards, these things gather to themselves — and it goes deep into their being, into the material, if you prefer to put it so, of which they are composed. It is we, the persons who are brought up, say for twenty years, along with these objects, who endow them, how could we do otherwise, with this inner life. We come up against them continually. We associate certain particular moments of our lives with them; with this one rather than with that one, and when, on perhaps the following day, we pass by the one against which this experience of ours has brushed its wings, the experience switches back full-fledged upon us, while all the feelings we had at that moment repeat themselves within us. All the chairs and tables and cupboards and book-cases and sideboards and chests-of-drawers and carpets and sofas and rugs and windowsills and staircases and mantelpieces in the house we live in or the room we live in are the recipients of the dominant emotions and major mental disturbances of our life, things that affect us not only before we go out into the elements of Nature or into the business of our day's work, but equally so when we return home after we have walked and climbed and ridden and driven, and after we have finished our day's job, whatever that job may be.

'Yes! the furniture of our dwelling is like the thousand and one material objects we pass each day on our way to our life's work. It collects our feelings and drinks them into itself. The arms of every armchair, the legs of every table, the knobs of every footstool, the edges of every cupboard, are collectors of human feelings; so you see it is quite impossible, unless you live in a completely bare room, and even then the walls, the floor, the ceiling, the window, the door, have their own intake — for the place where you have your feelings not to share these feelings with you.'

It was then that quite suddenly De Quincey rushed up to his Ann and carried her off by main force to share his interview with King Numa and with Egeria the king's Nymph in the cavern. Topsy and Turvy stared at each other in bewilderment. They didn't feel resentment or anger. But they felt disappointed. And Topsy felt frustrated by not being able to carry on her talk with Ann. By a heavenly stroke of good luck it was at this very moment that the Sea-Nymph Galatea, after a quarrel with her sister nymphs in the Pacific Ocean, burst into 'the Fourth Dimension', if that really was the proper name for this queer land of naked men and women. Angry with all her companion Nymphs in the deep Pacific Ocean was Galatea and it was only on the strength of her wrath that she had burst the barriers of normal life in our Universe and plunged into this unusual sphere. It was only on the strength of her flight up and out, with a mad desire to be where none of her usual companions could possibly find her, that she had burst into this strange world; and once here, with her desperation lost and her momentary madness vanished, it was natural enough that she drifted into touch with Topsy the moment she caught sight of her. The curious thing was that, in her fury with her companion-Nymphs, she had torn down from the wall of their 'House of Wings', one of their most sacred Temples of

Power, two of the most forcibly-feathered wings that were kept in that holy receptacle, and these she now recklessly offered to Topsy and Turvy. Galatea was bigger than either of them and much more strongly built and it would have been nothing to her to burst into the sacred cave of Egeria and to toss King Numa aside, as she offered that Nymph in Antro the means to escape. Little did she guess that Egeria, so far from wishing to leave her King, had but one desire, namely to help him to conquer the world. But Galatea had been deeply attracted to Topsy and she came up to them with such a winning smile and with so much of the mystery and magic of the depths of the Ocean about her that she quickly so enchanted them both that they agreed to fly straight back with her from prehistoric Rome to where this 'Fourth Dimension', or 'Dimension of Reality' touched the turnstile turning from which they had plunged into it. Under the protection of this formidable Sea-Nymph they neither of them had the slightest trepidation about being devoured by that Whirlwind and Whirlpool pair who lived in the chimney-top. So they both allowed her to affix to their bodies these spacious wings, which responded the moment they adhered to their naked shoulders to some interior muscular and fibrous power of assimilation that gave them the feeling that something within them had been long awaiting this moment.

Galatea seemed to know the way through the air across the whole length of the Dimension separating prehistoric Rome from modern London, and her two powerfully winged friends had no difficulty in following her. Indeed they felt as they flew how superior must be the lives of birds to the lives of men and animals. Walking with two legs, and still worse with four, struck them as comically humiliating as they swept through the sky and glanced at the various landscapes and seascapes that lay beneath them.

While these three were on their way Bibabug and Silly-suck, as they lay side by side on their bed, were engaged with their usual topic, the two points of which were Bibabug's shrinking from taking Sillysuck and Sillysuck's longing to have a baby. It was an extra warm night for that season of the year so they had left their house-door wide open as old Mr Bottom-Step had thumped his way round Turnstile Corner to buy a bottle of brandy. What therefore was their amazement when Topsy and Turvy arrived, followed by Galatea, whom they were both excitedly begging to enter the house with them. All three of them, all winged, came swishing in! The confusion was terrific. Everybody shouted at once; and, as might have been expected, Mr Brown Armchair and Mrs Grey Armchair, followed by Master Poker, came clattering downstairs to see what on earth had happened. Galatea the Sea-Nymph kept her wings neatly folded round her neck like a feathery scarf; but Topsy and Turvy carefully removed theirs and hung them up side by side on the wall. Galatea remained naked, save for her wings which played the part of a shawl, but both Topsy and Turvy, without even asking leave, searched Bibabug's and Sillysuck's cupboards till they found clothes that would fit them. During this incredible hubbub, roused to activity as he had never been in his whole life before, Bibabug seized Sillysuck, pulled her down upon the rug and there, while legs and skirts and boots and shoes were tripping and switching and stumbling over their bodies he violently, shamelessly, recklessly, desperately, ravished her and did so with such success that her muffled cry was a mixture of blood and tears and crazy exultation. 'I shall have a baby, a baby, a baby!' were the broken sounds that came up from the rug; but in the wild welter nobody heeded them.

Abertackle

1

The Abertackle folk were, it must be confessed, a queer lot. But then it must be remembered that Abertackle was itself a queer place; and queer places tend to breed queer people. It was the biggest hamlet in the Go Peninsula, a promontory that stretches out quite a long way into the sea and carries with it several rivers and estuaries that have been over-flowing their banks for thousands of years.

Why the dwellers in the Go Peninsula have never from time immemorial tried to build enough houses or to collect a big enough population to establish a town it is impossible to say. Visitors to the Go Peninsula, whether tourists or business men, will always tell you that they like the people there very much and find them hospitable and friendly, but what they never tell you for some mysterious reason is why they leave the place so quickly and rarely ever return to it.

Mr Charles Po and Mrs Mary Po, who were the oldest couple in Abertackle, lived in a comfortable little cottage called Crongy and were looked after by an elderly house-keeper called Nancy. 'I be afeared, mistress,' said this good-hearted competent lady one morning at the end of a rather cold February, 'that the master didn't like the sausages I cooked this morning. He hardly touched them; and yet his appetite is clearly all right for he eat as much bread and marmalade as he usually do.'

'Oh no, Nance,' said Mrs Po, 'he always speaks up when

he don't like a thing. The sausages are all right. I enjoyed
them, I ate every bit. If you ask me what I think it was, I
should say it was because I was telling him about Miss
Tarnt's asking me whether we'd go with her to Mrs
Thrapplewait's to lunch tomorrow. Miss Tarnt be always a
bit fearful of Mrs Thrapplewait's lunches because she likes
to ask Mr Willmop and you know what he is! So I was
telling the Master about this and asking if he minded going.
He don't like Mr Willmop for some reason. I expect the
Master remembers how when Mr Willmop once came to
tea here he said he didn't feel like having anything but bread
and butter when Master had gone to a deal of trouble
opening one of those American tins. Anyway, it was
because of something on his mind that the Master didn't eat
your sausages. He's funny like that, the Master is. I expect
all men are when it comes to table matters. They don't
know all the trouble folks are putting themselves to for their
sakes. Miss Tarnt be different from us ordinary folk in them
things. If she do want to do a thing she just do go and do it,
let come what may come! So it weren't only us having Mr
Willmop to deal with, it were being taken there by Miss
Tarnt. I guess t'were the fear of this tomorrow that made
the Master act funny about his meal and not eat his
sausages.'

Her mistress's words were evidently just the right ones to
soothe the hurt feelings of Nancy Potticup, for she went off
happily to the kitchen, thinking to herself: 'Well I be mighty
thankful that 'taint me as has to meet Mr Willmop tomorrow afternoon! I be feared I'd forget myself with him
and burst out at him!'

On the morning of the following day Mr Ernest Willmop
allowed himself to sleep late. He had told his housekeeper,
Titty Tinkle, for Mr Willmop was a bachelor of about fifty,
not to bring him his cup of tea at eight and that she needn't
bother about breakfast till he came downstairs. He knew
that when she heard him moving about his room she would
begin to prepare the breakfast he liked best, which was

always the same, fried eggs and bacon and several cups of coffee.

'What a damnably bloody business it is,' thought Ernest Willmop, 'to be alive on this confounded Earth! But it's no good saying that. We've all got to go through with it till we're dead.' Ernest Willmop was a very powerful tall man with brown curly hair and fierce dark eyes. 'It isn't,' he said to himself, 'that I hate everything that's alive. It's human beings I hate, creatures on two legs, human beings and monkeys! I like horses and cattle very well and sheep and lambs too. Why the devil did we go and climb trees and build houses and barns and sheds and walls? And then all this awful cooked food. Why can't we eat bread and oatmeal and apples and pears and nuts and have none of this blasted cookery? Oh how much nicer sheep and cattle and horses and ponies are than men and monkeys! I don't mind babies and I don't mind women so much, when they have babies. No! I don't mind women and children. It's men and monkeys I hate; and when women behave like men and monkeys I hate them too! Well, I've got to go to lunch at Mrs Thrapplewait's today and I've got to meet Miss Tarnt there and Mr and Mrs Po too, so I mustn't have breakfast too late or I shan't be able to touch a mouthful of this blasted lunch.'

Ernest Willmop did manage, in spite of his angry mutterings as he hurried there after his late breakfast, to devour quite a satisfactory lot of Mrs Thrapplewait's feast. This chivalrous behaviour as he munched and swallowed was in a considerable measure due to his interest in Miss Tarnt whose own share of the Thrapplewaitian spread, or at any rate her own interest in it, consisted in making a map on her plate of France and Spain and Portugal by the aid of the spikes of her silver fork and the various edibles so far uneaten.

Yes, there was something about Miss Tarnt that had a singular effect upon Ernest Willmop. 'She's like me,' he thought, 'completely independent of the whole confounded lot of them and absolutely indifferent to what anyone thinks about her.'

Miss Tarnt was only twenty-five but she looked over thirty. She had thin dark hair, pale greenish-blue eyes, an aquiline nose and a pointed chin. It was only when somebody said something to her in a tone of affectionate respect that her expression softened a little. When she talked to the company at large it was always on the same topic, the superiority of the age of their grandparents and great-grandparents over their own age. Mrs Thrapplewait was a tiny little old lady, very thin and with features such as a child might have drawn if it had wanted to draw a fairy grandmother; for her nose, mouth and eyes were very small but the lines about them and between them and her ears and throat and across her high forehead were so deep that when she concentrated her gaze upon anyone in particular that person, if a sensitive person, felt as if he or she had become a little wavering, flickering, quivering, bodiless wrinkle, floating in the air between her listening mind and the lecturing mind of her interlocutor.

'Mr Po thinks,' said Mrs Po to Mrs Thrapplewait, 'that he found this morning the first celandine of the year. It's the last day of February today, isn't it?'

'Oh no, Mrs Po!' cried the little old lady eagerly, 'it's only the twenty-eighth, and it's leap year! So you don't know what it says in the Bible — "Leap year coming once in four, gives to February one day more!" '

'It doesn't say that in the Bible, my good woman, it's only an old country-saying,' put in Mr Po. 'But it's perfectly true. It's tomorrow, not today, that is the last day of February. Do you think that people have often found a celandine before February was over?'

'No I guess not,' replied their hostess. But her expression was so vague and so dazed and so bewildered that Mrs Po felt afraid that her husband's rebuke had troubled the old lady's mind. 'I wish,' thought Mrs Po, 'that he hadn't said "my good woman" for that isn't a nice way to address a lady we're lunching with.'

The thoughts of Mr Po were running in a different channel. 'I expect I was a fool,' he thought, 'to settle in Abertackle; though Crongy is a nice cottage and the walks round here suit me very well. But I'd like the place better if Mary had given me a few children to walk with me. She has to stay in the house, I know, to make sure that old Nancy isn't treating half the tramps in the place to meals in the kitchen. But my walks were much more enjoyable in those old days at Crockover when Mary and I used to explore the place together. Of course we had Parson Ratrap to deal with then, but after that day I brought Cousin Tony to church with me and Ratrap found out he was a lord, the fellow quieted down.'

Neither Mr nor Mrs Po, nor indeed Ernest Willmop himself, whose hatred of everybody never prevented him from catching the special quirks and quibbles and cranks and whimsies and oddities of any particular person he met, failed to miss the peculiar relation that existed between a gentleman in the Go Peninsula who was always called Squire Neverbang, and another gentleman who lived with him. These two persons were met by Mr and Mrs Po as they walked home that afternoon, and the four of them not only shook hands but were persuaded by Squire Neverbang to enter a little café called the Clapper-Cove and enjoy a cup of coffee.

'What do you think of the way this chap Willmop goes barging about abusing everybody?' enquired Mr Po addressing Ooly-Fooly, Squire Neverbang's companion. Ooly-Fooly had been a famous European clown from the age of fifteen to the age of twenty-four. Then something happened to him the details of which, though gossip and scandal have derived exquisite satisfaction from turning the mystery of this something over and over and over and over, have never really been brought to light. Was it a normal love affair? We very likely will never know. Perhaps it was no love affair at all. Perhaps it was something to do with his mentality. Perhaps he suddenly made the discovery that he had gone mad. Perhaps he had discovered to his horror that he had been mad ever since some secret mental shock which he had never revealed.

'I think,' he said now, 'what Willmop really wants is to be challenged in the old-fashioned manner to a duel! Would you let me challenge him, Squire?'

'Oh no,' threw in Mrs Po. 'I know Willmop well enough to know that he'd treat such a challenge with ribald and vulgar contempt. I think what he really wants is a good hiding from someone who has the power to give it to him and the power to make him hold his tongue about it afterwards.'

It was then that to the astonishment of everybody Miss Tarnt and Mr Willmop entered the café together.

The landlord of the Clapper-Cove Café , whose name was Dick Underhead, was a big burly man who had one of those brains that clever people never understand and that stupid people always understand. 'How wonderful,' he now vociferated as if he had been the manager of a game of charades at a Public School, ready in a moment to set them off spouting like the frogs of Aristophanes, Krekekekex. Ko! Ax! Ko! Ax! Krekekekex! Ko! Ax! — 'how wonderful to have all the learned people of Abertackle in my little show-place!'

' 'Tisn't a show place, silly man,' said Miss Tarnt. 'It's an eat-and-drink place. It's a restaurant. Give us your best coffee and what you feel goes with it best! What *does* go with it best? You ought to know, Mr Underhead.'

There was something in her tone as she said this that pleased the burly host of the Clapper-Cove. He had the wit to see that Miss Tarnt was no ordinary pub-frequenting girl. He walked round behind the bar for a bit and then came back holding a couple of paper-bags in his hand. Then he himself sat down beside Miss Tarnt, before whom the barmaid, a plump little wench with a mischievous laugh, had already put a plate and a coffee pot and a double-handled mug.

'Get me a mug, Kitty,' he said, 'and some more coffee and I'll explain everything to the lady. And get the same for Mr Willmop and ask him if he wants milk and sugar.'

Mr Willmop was so noisily explicit on the subject of what he wanted that Dick Underhead was able to give Miss Tarnt, beside whom he seemed to have established himself for the night, a private little lecture on the biscuits that went best with coffee.

'My husband found a celandine today in the rocks up the hill. Have either of you found one yet?' Mrs Po addressed this remark to both Squire Neverbang and Ooly-Fooly by way of making friendly conversation.

Ooly answered it blithely. 'No, madam, neither Squire nor I are flower-lovers or flower-discoverers. What we do see when we walk out are the mountains and the rivers and the sea and the sky. Yes, it's Nature in the large, not the little–tittle–fittle–wittle–spittle blossoms or leaves coming out that interest us.'

Squire Neverbang let his pet fool speak for them both, not only because it always tickled his fancy to hear what Ooly would say, but also because he had to greet two fresh customers entering Dick Underhead's café. These were Jack Coffiny and Tom Boundary, the well-bred gentlemen who behaved as if they were brothers though really they were only cousins.

2

Jack Coffiny was thinking to himself: 'I should never have dared to come into this place alone; but with Tom I seem to be able to go anywhere. Isn't it quaint how frightened I am of people and how I love the moment they start asking me about my *Philosophy of Escape*. Tom asked me just now how many books I've written on this subject and he didn't seem a bit surprised when I told him it must be more than a dozen. Oh I do pray that when he asked me last night before we went to bed to sum up in as few words as possible what my message to the world really was I did put it right. I think I told him that our whole human life was, if we consider it mentally, apart from what we have to do and how we have to act, in the ordinary course of each day, a frantic struggle to escape from the old traditional legends and myths and customs and convictions and symbols and ideas and moralities and ethics and religion and idolatries and popular beliefs. I tried to explain that there is no mental reason why we should believe in either God or the Devil. I told him that because Jesus was the greatest man who ever lived, as I verily believe he was, there is no reason for thinking that every single thing he said or thought was an absolute truth. Indeed, doesn't his own cry from the Cross about God forsaking him prove that he had made the great mistake of his life by believing in God? Oh I do so pray to Jesus and to old warlike Jehovah, the tribal god of the Jews that I did manage to make clear to Tom what the real essence of my

Philosophy of Escape amounted to: namely that we must shake off all mythology, all religion, all worship of God, all dogmatic and explicit ideas of the nature of another life. We must escape, I explained to him, every fancy about another life after death. The final escape, I told him, must be indeed an escape from life itself, from any sort of life, an escape into the divine nothingness of death.'

Tom Boundary was thinking as, led by Jack Coffiny, he shook hands with the Squire and Ooly-Fooly and with Charles and Mary Po and with Willmop and Miss Tarnt, that he wished he hadn't to spend his time in this confounded café when he might be practising bowling and batting on the newly-rolled field where they had had nets set up so as to be able to practise at any hour of the day. 'If he doesn't want to practise batting when we're down there tomorrow I won't bother him with it. We'll go down there late in the afternoon when the club's watching that match with the county's second eleven.'

How often does it happen in life that two of the best friends in the world when confronted by a group of other friends indulge in thoughts directly opposite! Tom Boundary would have been absolutely astonished had he known what thoughts were passing through Jack Coffiny's peculiar mind at that moment. And yet they were thoughts that Jack Coffiny had had since he was a child. He was thinking to himself: 'What a funk I am! What an incredible coward I am! I should never be in this café at all, talking to all these good people, if it weren't for Tom. And yet if they were a group of the undergrads of Cambridge preparing for a debate with the undergrads of Oxford on the topic whether God exists or not, Oxford saying he does and Cambridge saying he doesn't, I shouldn't be scared at all. In fact I'd be in an extra happy mood. I'd soon be showing these Oxonians that it's as silly to believe in the kind of God we are told to believe in as it is to believe that Gaia, the Earth, gave Cronos, or Saturn, the jagged pieces of flint to cut out the testicles of Ouranos or Uranus that were the cause of all the titanic monsters to whom she was forced to give birth. But we must remember that there are episodes in the New Testament quite as moving and as touching as anything in the Old Testament; and we must remember that the birth of Venus Aphrodite out of the sea-foam caused by the dismemberment of Ouranos has a mysterious beauty in it which carries us away beyond any merciful or merciless mutilation.'

While these encounters were taking place, and these thoughts were floating around in the Clapper-Cove Café, Miss Nelly Saunter and Lady Astis were approaching the cottage of Mr Bob Ord and Mrs Letty Ord, who had invited them to tea.

Mr Bob Ord had been helping his wife to spread the bread and butter and arguing with her about whether they ought to provide two kinds of jam for their visitors or only one. 'What I think myself,' said Mr Bob Ord, 'is that it's best to give them only one kind of jam. Do you suppose that what people want when they don't know you at all is to know all they can about you and your various peculiarities? Of course it isn't. What they want is to tell you all their ways and tastes and peculiar personal interests. What they want, in other words, is to use you as something to bang upon and knock upon and hammer upon so that they can hear the echoes. And what is the echo they are after? *The echo of themselves!* Yes, that is what they want. With our habitual companions, who have had all the occasions, all the chances, all the opportunities they can possibly want there is now no more to be got out of us in the way of responsive echoes. They may tap and knock at the cabinets of peculiarity from which they want to get a reverberation or a sigh or groan of response, or at least a tinkle; but they get nothing but dead silence.'

Lady Astis and Miss Nelly Saunter had long been close friends; and recently, for they both had small fixed incomes, they had decided to share a cottage in Abertackle. They both had eccentric tastes, though in rather different ways, and something about the quaintness and oddity of Bob Ord and Letty Ord had appealed to them both very strongly the moment they met them.

'The great thing,' said Lady Astis as they approached the street door of the Ords, 'is to avoid like the devil making them angry with each other. Old Bob is always saying things, calculated, I should have thought, to make any woman furious; but Letty is curiously forbearing. I suppose she knows old Bob so well that she has come to accept his cross-grained outbursts as part of her life. That's a sign of a wise woman, isn't it, Nelly? Men are as they are and apparently very difficult to change, however much we may try. Of course we aren't like that at all; and we soon get to know each other so well that —'

She interrupted herself by ringing the bell of 'Tickety-top', as the Ords' cottage was called. She did this with a smile so familiar to Nelly Saunter that it finished her remark without words.

'Oh here you are!' cried Letty Ord, opening the door. 'Bob was just saying he thought he saw you coming. He can see up and down the lane from our window which is often —' She too, just as Lady Astis had done with her words, completed her sentence with the welcoming sound of the door closing behind them. In a moment they had got their galoshes and jackets off; and the four of them were seated at a little square table enjoying cup after cup of tea and piece after piece of thin bread and butter with all the jam anybody could want spread daintily with little silver knives, one for each of them.

'I saw quite a lot of people,' said Bob Ord, 'go into Clapper-Cove Café. I wonder if old Underhead had enough drink saved up in his cellar to satisfy them.'

'I'm perfectly sure he had,' said Lady Astis.

'He's a crafty old time-server,' said Nelly Saunter. 'But I like him all the same. Do you remember, Susan?' (this remark was addressed to Lady Astis) 'how amusing he was when we took little Tottie Tender to have a glass of cider there? He behaved so nicely to her. I had a letter from her only a week ago in which she spoke of him. Uncle Paul took her with him to Geneva, which is full of our relations and they all were so sweet to her. She's back in Arundel now, where Uncle Paul has a life's job at the Castle. She was there on her birthday and when the Duke talked to her she begged him to give her *Alice in Wonderland* for a birthday present and the Duke gave her an old copy of his own which he'd kept since he was little. She wrote to me such a pretty letter about it, telling me she keeps it in her bedroom near her bed.'

'I've always thought,' said Bob Ord, 'that the time will come when people will be afraid to speak of machinery without reverently lowering their voices as we do now when we speak of God or the Holy Ghost. They are inventing calculating machines that have the same power of thought as a human brain, only they are less likely to be led astray. A time will probably soon come when this Earth will be ruled by a group of machines, one British, one French, one German, one American, one Spanish, one Portuguese, one Australian, one African, one Icelandic, one Canadian, and after that there will perhaps be a vast Eternal Machine that will rule not only this present Universe but all the Universes that the Life Force may create in the future.'

Whether it was the thought of Bob Ord's Eternal Machine or whether Lady Astis had come to the conclusion from watching her friend's face that Nelly was growing too nervous from listening to all this, she rose up from her chair, helped Nelly to rise by a gentle uplift of her sleeve, and told the Ords that there was a risk of some friends of theirs from London looking in before supper-time, so that they would have to go at once. She shook hands with them both in such a lively and grateful manner that it saved Nelly from anything but a quick handshake.

When the front door was shut behind her Letty Ord said to Bob Ord, 'You bet your life it was your machine talk that hurried them off.'

'No, I don't think so,' said Bob to Letty. 'I think the Lady thought her friend was feeling ill.'

A day or two after this little tea-party at the Ords', Miss Tarnt was returning with a full basket from a shopping excursion when she met in a little side-street Squire Never-bang's friend Mr Ooly-Fooly, who was evidently enjoying the sensation of being by himself without any special purpose or any imperative undertaking. The whole look, appearance, manner and expression of the man seemed to say to the ground beneath his feet and to the air around him and to the sky above his head: 'Oh how heavenly it is to be free from every mortal person you know and every practical thing to be done and everything in the past to remember and everything in the future to consider! To come loitering down a road like this with no one to love and no one to hate and no purpose to think of, with nothing but the road to travel on, the air to breathe, the sky to gaze at and no sensation in your whole body and no thought in your whole mind except the feeling of being happily alone, is this not far better than any paradise we are told of or any fairyland we have invented? Could anything in heaven or earth be better? Oh how delicious not even to have to think why it's so delicious!'

3

Miss Tarnt was overjoyed to meet Mr Ooly-Fooly alone like this. The moment she caught sight of him she said to herself: 'I'm always being led on by my own silly mania for men who seem to me quite different from all other men. And here indeed is one, as anyone can see in a moment, who is completely different from all others, and yet I know him as well as I know anybody in Abertackle! Isn't it funny that I've never got him to know me! I believe I *could* get him to be quite intimate with me. Perhaps meeting him like this alone in the street and just before twilight begins is an encounter designed especially for us by Providence itself! But I can hardly walk about the town alone with him, can I? Besides, I've walked too much already. I'm tired. I want to go home and rest. And I certainly wouldn't be at my best in talk, unless we could sit down. Oh, but *that*'s a good idea. I've thought of it. Why don't I ask him to have a cup of tea with me at the Cokesy-Wokesy? Aunt Ora's always glad to see me there. In fact I helped her to invent that cosy name for her and Miss Evercan's tiny tea-shop. Yes! Yes! Oh yes! I'll take him to Cokesy-Wokesy and we'll have a lovely talk with Aunt Ora and Miss Evercan.'

She had no difficulty at all in persuading Ooly-Fooly to accompany her. It was indeed just the sort of thing that suited him at the moment; for happy though he was at being alone he had begun to feel a little hungry and thirsty.

Miss Tarnt and Ooly-Fooly were lucky. Nobody but its

two owners were in the Cokesy-Wokesy when they
arrived. Aunt Ora and Miss Evercan were enjoying their
freedom from customers by having a game of cards all to
themselves on one of the little tables. They jumped to their
feet, and the moment they saw who had opened the door
they both cried with delight: 'Oh! it's you! Oh! it's you!' and
seating them both at the table where they had been playing
they switched the cards away and tidied the table-cloth.

'How's Squire Neverbang?' enquired Aunt Ora.

'Oh, he's all right!' replied Ooly-Fooly. 'He's always all
right. I wish I had something of his portentous calm. Do
you know what he began last night?' Both Aunt Ora and
Miss Evercan gazed eagerly at Ooly-Fooly.

'No! do tell us!' cried Miss Evercan.

'No! do tell us!' cried Aunt Ora.

Miss Tarnt looked pleasantly round the tea-shop. So far
from being jealous of the way her companion had monopo-
lized the interest of the two ladies she felt thankful to be with
such a monopolizer. She always preferred to be an onlooker
and a listener to taking the lead in anything that went on
within a house. When it became a matter of being out of
doors and of exploring the countryside or following any of
the estuary banks of the Go Peninsula or taking a climb up
Mount Gogglewog Miss Tarnt was always the one to take
the lead.

'Do you know what I think?' said Ooly-Fooly.

'No!' cried both their hostesses with one voice.

'I think,' said Ooly-Fooly, 'that we ought to start a little
theatre in Abertackle. There are so many folk here who
come crowding round every wireless and every telly, and
we've got so many clever couples like Mr and Mrs Po and
such real geniuses at comedy and tragedy like my friend
Squire Neverbang, and not a few born clowns like my lone
self, that it seems silly and wasteful not to start a real proper
Little Theatre here that would give us all something exciting
to concentrate on and use our dramatic abilities on. What do
you think, Aunt Ora? What do you think, Miss Evercan?'

Aunt Ora replied without a second's hesitation: 'I'm all for it, Mr Fooly! I'm all for it!'

And Miss Evercan replied also, though in a less excited tone, 'Yes, I agree entirely with such an idea; but we'd have to have stage-directors and ballet-mistresses and so forth, shouldn't we? I mean people who know more about the stage than we do, wouldn't we? and people who know how to cope with men and women in their separate characteristics?'

'But men and women are both human beings aren't they?' threw in Miss Evercan.

'They're different sorts of human beings,' went on Ooly-Fooly. 'I've been studying the difference between them very carefully and not only in regard to one having a penis to push up the hole in front of the other's body till it makes the other bleed by the loss of her virginity; but in the fact that the one has breasts with nipples so as to suckle babies and the other only little pink dots where a woman's two breasts are, though of course both of them have the same little dark scar in the centre of their human stomachs. But if you want to know the greatest difference in their ways by which you can always distinguish them I will tell you this. You never see a man touch his face. If he has a beard and a moustache he may give each of them a good pull now and again. But if he has no hair on his face at all he never touches it. But every woman and every girl is constantly touching her face. You watch them. You watch the one you live with. You'll soon see her hand go up to her face. It's just as if they thought that at any moment some delicate little flower, like a daisy or snowdrop, might suddenly start growing out of their face. But whatever the cause of their doing it may be, the fact remains that you can't look at any woman or girl for a minute or two without seeing her hand go up to her face.'

Ooly-Fooly stopped haranguing them and looked from the face of Aunt Ora to the face of Miss Evercan with a questioning eagerness.

But it was his companion Miss Tarnt who commented on his eloquent oration. 'What we all must remember,' said Miss Tarnt wisely, 'is the fact that neither a man nor a woman created this world, nor — I speak as what they call a free-thinker — did some mysterious Being called God create it. It was — I speak as an unbeliever — created by what we call the life-force or that energy in the heart of Nature which drives everything to grow and to become more and more alive, that energy which at the beginning must have driven Man to come out of the sea and to climb up trees, that energy which is at this very moment suggesting to us through the receptive and porous mind of my friend Mr Fooly that we start a Little Theatre in Abertackle like that first and foremost of all Little Theatres which Maurice Browne started in the Middle West of America.'

'But the point is, my dear Miss Tarnt,' cried Aunt Ora eagerly, 'this adventurous energy you speak of is not confined to the creation of Group Movements and Organized Undertakings such as Little Theatres and Borough Committees: it shows itself in us, in ourselves, in the secret soul of each of us men and women individually. And don't you think there may be a faint danger that when we feel this urge within us to action on our own account, and then being, as most of us are, a bit nervous of striking out on our own, we may be tempted by the existence of a Little Theatre or a Borough Committee to dodge this imperative urge from within, which is surely much more in harmony with the energy in all Nature of which we're speaking than any group design like a Little Theatre or a Borough Committee?'

It is extraordinary how we are all affected by currents of feeling in the air originating from sources totally unknown to us. At this moment a weird surge of delight welled up in the heart of Miss Tarnt who was, you must remember, still nearer twenty than thirty, as she gazed at her pick-up, Ooly-Fooly. 'He, anyway,' she thought, 'will be, as long as he lives, whether Squire Neverbang is his companion or a

4

Miss Tarnt's lodging wasn't far from Squire Neverbang's
house where Ooly-Fooly lived, so they walked together
through the evening streets to that edifice, for it was a large
dwelling, and said goodnight at the door. Miss Tarnt felt
she could have kissed Ooly-Fooly, for she had taken a real
liking to him; but she didn't dare to take such a risk just
then. Besides, Squire Neverbang might have been
watching from some upper window. So she just tapped him
on his hand with her bare knuckles. 'We'll have tea again
there, won't we?' she said. And though all he said was 'Sure
we will, my dear!' she derived a curious and special satisfaction from his calling her 'my dear', as if they were friends
of quite long standing. When she reached her lodging she
wasn't sorry to find her landlady, Dilly Dally, standing at
the foot of the stairs.

'I've taken up your cup of tea,' she said, 'I've left it by
your bed. I knew you'd be back by eight and wouldn't want
more than one cup. But I thought you'd like just that one,
after being out to a regular tea-party. Did all go well? They
are a funny pair, that couple of old spinning-wheels. But I
confess I have myself a sneaking fondness for them. Anyway they've as good a basketful of naughty tales about old
folk in Abertackle as you can hear anywhere else! I like Aunt
Ora the best. Which do you like the best?'

Miss Tarnt pondered thoughtfully. Then she said, 'Were
you christened Dilly, my dear? It goes so well with Dally

that anybody'd think they went together and that your real name was Brown or Smith or Jones or Green or Robinson. Yes, I like Aunt Ora the best. But I like Miss Evercan too. I love both the dear old things. Do you think, my dear, that when you and I get as old as they are we'll be as nice a pair of old knitikins as they are? Oh yes, Dilly, but do for the Lord's sake tell me whether you were christened just for the sport of making it go with Dally?'

Miss Dilly Dally looked smilingly at her lodger. 'No, my dear,' she said. 'My old dad, Jeremiah Dally, was a Jewish Rabbi in Birmingham. He and Mother were both killed in the blitz in the war, when I would have been too, only Cousin Tuckerin had taken me to the shop where they sold fancy-dress dolls. Cousin Tuckerin always said that in war-time the best thing for mothers to do was to nurse babies in the parlour and the best thing for girls to do was to nurse dolls by the nursery fender. Mother's name was Abigail and I never have forgotten how she taught me to read the Bible. She made me read it, the Old Testament I mean, from beginning to end. Mother and Father were killed when I'd got to the forty-seventh chapter of Isaiah. And I've never read a line since then.'

'Do tell me, Dilly,' said Miss Tarnt, 'who that young couple are you've got now in the basement?'

'Oh *them*,' cried Dilly Dally. 'I'll tell you all about them when I bring up your cup of tea in a few minutes. Then you'll have something to dream about! I'll be taking down their supper to them presently.'

Miss Tarnt went upstairs to her bedroom; and in about half an hour when she had already got her dressing-gown on and every thing else except her nightgown off, her landlady kept her word; and while they shared a cup of tea sitting on the bed she told her about the couple in the basement.

'The boy,' she said, 'is Bickery Bum and the girl is Fanny Flabbergast. Their love-story is a quaint and touching one. Bickery was an assistant gamekeeper on the estate of Squire

Neverbang. He had to be always on the look-out for poachers; not only four-legged ones, such as badgers and foxes, but two-legged ones such as greedy and acquisitive rascals from the slums of the Go Peninsula. Fanny Flabbergast came of a well-known literary family in Valentia and was a clever girl who had earned quite a considerable income from teaching English in a Paris girls' school. In the Go Peninsula she was fond of taking long walks by the banks of one of the estuaries, all of which led eventually out to sea. It was on one of these very walks that she encountered Bickery, who was a skilled fisherman and caught dace and roach and perch and sometimes even a pike in the Go estuaries. They were attracted to each other at once and in summer time lots of Abertackle townspeople would get accustomed to meeting them; she carrying bunches of wild flowers and he carrying his rod and the fish he had caught. It was our clergyman, one Reverend Squot, who must have put it into their heads to get married. He confided to me once, for though a bachelor, he liked talking to females, and I think he derived quite a smattering of naughty and mischievous delight from telling me about it, that when Bickery and Fanny asked him whether it was right for them to partake of Holy Communion at Church when they had been making love to each other he had replied that if they were engaged to be married it was perfectly and absolutely all right. Sex-play, he told them, is entirely justifiable in the eyes of God if it is going to last, and above all if it is going to result in children. "I", he told them, "am the representative of God on Earth." I remember being so shocked when one Sunday I found Bickery embracing Fanny in a mossy glen and making love to her on our ground in a way that fully displayed their sexual excitement that I cried, "I am the representative of God upon Earth and as God I command you to be officially and formally engaged to be married." They listened to the Reverend Squot's words obediently with the result that in a week or two he married them and gave them Holy Communion.

5

'Life seems growing stranger and stranger every day,' said Mr Charles Po to Mrs Mary Po as they sat by their drawing-room fire a few days after Miss Tarnt and Ooly-Fooly came to tea with Aunt Ora and Miss Evercan. 'I wonder if we did right in letting things happen like that.'

'Don't talk like that, Charley,' protested Mary Po. 'You've forgotten how it was and how difficult they were to manage. Do remember, my dear, how carefully we argued it all out that evening in June after that dreadful afternoon when Gor was so rude that you boxed his ears and he snatched Nelly up in his arms and carried her out; and when I called after him, "Where are you taking her?" he only shouted back those terrible words that are always returning to me in my dreams, "over the hills and far away!" I know you were right to be angry with him and box his ears. Most fathers would have given him a sound flogging, but it was so cruel of him to take little Nelly off with him. She was only thirteen you know and girls of that age —'

'Don't talk about it any more, my dear!' groaned Mr Po.

'Gor was a queer child from his babyhood up. You never could tell what he'd do next or say next. We must remember this, my dear, anyway — Nelly loved him intensely, desperately, far more than she loved either of us.'

'But isn't that *incest*, Mary dear?' said Charley Po gravely.

'I don't know what it is!' cried his wife, 'and I'm sure dear little Nelly didn't either! When a young girl of her age falls in love she thinks of nothing but the youth she loves. Gor loved her too. He'll look after her, you can depend on that. He'll fight for her, work for her, slave for her. I'm not exaggerating, my dear Charley. Don't think that for a moment. He loved her just as you loved me when we first met and you were seventeen and I was fifteen.'

'But oh I wish, my dear,' groaned Mr Po, 'that I hadn't boxed his ears. But after what he said to me — yes, to both of us, what else could I do? If I'd behaved like that when I was a boy my father would have given me a sound thrashing.'

'No! but think, my dear Charley, here we are, two elderly people in our seventies and how lovely it would have been to have Gor and Nelly to look after us! They ran away from us because we didn't properly understand them; because we frightened them, because we were too severe with them.'

'Well, my dear Mary,' said Charley Po, 'you must remember I did all I could do to find out where they had gone. But nobody had seen them, nobody in the whole of Abertackle that I could find or hear of; nobody in the whole of the Go Peninsula. You must give me credit for a great deal of unpleasant effort and a great many unpleasant encounters and interviews. I did my very utmost. But they were gone, just as Gor called back to you: "over the hills and far away".'

To Charles Po's astonishment his wife rose to her feet. 'I can't listen to any more of your excuses, my dear,' she cried indignantly. 'If you hadn't boxed Gor's ears that day they would both be with us now. Heaven bestowed those two children upon us in spite of all our sins; and instead of bringing them up properly or trying to understand them we allowed a great gap to yawn bigger and bigger and bigger between them and us. We were too severe with them, too narrow with them, too traditional and conventional with them. We ought to have got it lodged in our pair of stupid heads that both the world and our life in the world has to

move forward. There is something in this existence of ours
— call it what you will — that refuses to stop moving on,
yes, refuses to let what they call evolution be hindered and
weighed down and loaded up by obstinate stupidity and
foolish clinging to all the old things. Many a night, when
you were busy reading Jeremy Taylor or Sir Thomas
Browne or *The Anatomy of Melancholy* or *Robinson Crusoe* or
Middlemarch or *Finnegans Wake*, our son Gor would be ex-
pounding to me the most original, the most daring, the
newest and most unexpected theories about the nature of
matter and these atoms and monads and neutrons and all
those other things we read about in the daily papers and that
of course I don't understand a thing about. But Gor did!
Yes, he did! You should have heard all the ideas he told me
about! Of course he was too awed by his father's presence
and by the old tradition of respect for his father to rattle
away like that to you. But I swear to you, my dear, if you'd
heard him you would have been impressed just as I was.'

It had been very natural indeed that anyone should have
acquired such an admiration for Gor but it was also in-
evitable that it should have ended, or, let me say, should
have been interrupted, in the way it was, because Gor was
essentially such a peculiar and original youth and the
motions of his mind were so deeply born and so violently
outflung that nothing could make you sure what he would
be up to next. Gor's waist was small but his arms were long
for his age; and his hips were broad and muscular; and you
felt as you watched him that he could respond not only to
any physical challenge by leaping in any direction, but so
massive was his forehead and so intelligent his deep-sunk
eyes that you could not help feeling that whatever mental
appeal you made to him would meet with the exact response you wanted.

As a matter of fact it was under a low arch in a corner of
Hyde Park Gardens in London that young Gor was resting
that afternoon while he pondered on the great undertaking
he had decided to begin that day. Yes, young Gor now was

'Yes! I, Gor, am now starting on my career from London, although my home is in Abertackle, in the Go Peninsula. I have learnt to walk on air with the aid of a stick and I am now setting out with the intention of walking round the Sun and the Moon and all the various stars near them of which we get glimpses, including the group to which we have given the name of Orion's Belt. This is for me, Gor, the start of my career. How it will end the spirits of the air will know better than I ever shall. Oh what a thing Life is! And what a thing Death is!

'Well, here I am,' he repeated to himself. 'And I don't feel a touch of dyspepsia on my left side nor a touch of duodenal hurting me on my right side where my new trouble, some bad little growth, must have developed. But I am really beginning my true career.'

Deeper and deeper darkness soon began to surround him as the evening became night and so cloudy a night that it was not long before the moon followed the sun; and most of the little glittering stars followed the moon into extinction. Not all of them at once, however, nor was Gor displeased at catching a glimpse of one or two of these little gleaming jewels at intervals. At least they gave him a reassurance that he was doing what he wanted to do, that is to say whirl round the whole astronomical galaxy that surrounded the Earth, where he had been born and brought up, and indicating that he was pursuing the course he had proposed for himself and that he had followed in his imagination night after night. So he went hurrying through the darkness, striding at something like a run with his big stick clutched tight in his right hand. It was when he reached the darkest spot in his circular advance that he met young Maia Tuffalon. They both stopped and stood stone-still staring in bewilderment at each other.

'Where are you going?' said Gor to Maia.

'Where have you come from?' said Maia to Gor.

'Abertackle's my home,' said Gor. 'But I've come from London. Where is your home?'

'I too come from London,' said Maia. 'But my home is in Portland.'

'Near Portland Bill?' enquired Gor.

'Oh no!' cried Maia. 'Near Chesil Beach.'

'Have you a mother and father?' enquired Gor.

'No,' replied Maia. 'I have only got great-grandmother Tweedle-Weedle. We live alone together in Tickery-Wickery Villa, a nice big comfortable house where our people have lived for a hundred years. Have you got a father and mother?'

'To tell you the honest truth, my dear girl, I have run away from them. I have a sister whom I love so much that I have hidden her away from our father and mother, hidden her under the care of an old naval captain for whom she cares as if he were her uncle. I often go to see her. I often sleep in their house. I do envy you, my dear friend, your great-grandmother. I'd give half the money I've got — and it's only a little — to have even a grandmother.'

Evidently delighted to have aroused this handsome young man's envy, Maia Tuffalon tried to increase it. 'My great-granny,' she hastened to tell him, 'had a brother who lived at St Ives and had several wives, but his wives were all alive and lived with him still. He loved to tell his old sister that he was a poly-something. I forget how to spell the word but I remember he was mighty proud of being whatever it was and whenever he went along the London road he would take his ladies with him as if they were so many schoolgirls.'

7

'You will come on with me?' said Gor to Maia. 'You can take my arm when you feel tired.' Maia smiled. 'I don't want to leave you yet. But unlike you I don't go on by any steady movements. I go by sudden inspiration.'

It was at that moment that they were overtaken by a person whom both of them knew; for he was famous in that part of the country, namely David Cox, the painter. He was being carried through the air by a space-horse, a creature about whom all the local legends were full but whom few actual persons had ever seen. This particular space-horse who now brought Cox quite close to them was different from others of his kind in that he had a horn, a knotted twisted horn.

'Where are you two going?' Cox enquired of them.

'Exploring space,' replied Gor.

'A night or two ago,' said Cox, 'I couldn't sleep. I had been painting several forest scenes, none of which pleased me. I dreamt that if I went on the following Friday to one of the paths I had painted I should find a child's toy chariot harnessed to a space-horse which would be ready to take me anywhere. So when that day came, dream-drugged I recklessly set out and settled in my boy's chariot and whipping up its space-horse off I went. But I never thought I'd meet Gor of Gordale or Maia of Go Peninsula!'

Thus speaking, as Homer would say, the painter Cox

waved his whip like a flag and all three of them, Gor and Maia with Cox leading, went off round the world.

Oddly enough, in their interest at being three against the whole bulk of Space none of them realized the personal significance of those horns on the space-horse's head. This lack of insight was by no means unobserved by the alert consciousness of the brain out of which these horns were projected, the brain in fact of none other than the Devil himself. 'Oh,' thought he, 'how incredibly stupid human beings are! Nor is this confounded space-horse into whose being I have entered much more intelligent than the silly girl and these two idiotic men. My old fussy enemy God became as stupid as this before he died. Fancy his being able to invent and manufacture all he did out of empty space, sun, moon, earth and stars, and not being able to prevent old age making him dotty and helpless. I confess I miss the old fool. After all, I owe him my life. He invented me. Shall I get old and idiotic as he did? I wonder if it is possible, as I heard one of them say to another not many days ago, that some clever scientific individual will arise one day and invent a new world more intricate and remarkable even than old God's world now? I hope I'll still be alive on that day. But maybe not. Prophesying is one of the arts that have passed away. What also will have passed away will be the human traditional imagination as to what I am thinking about behind these horns of mine. The general idea no doubt is that I am rejoicing about the death of God — that is to say if the news of that event has already swallowed up the old idea that it was impossible for God to die. But if I were to blurt out now without any hesitation all that I am actually thinking, how completely different all the mortal creatures now alive on the earth and in the sun and moon and every one of these glittering stars would find it from all that they are imagining! As I say, they are imagining that I am going over in my mind every detail of God's death. They are imagining that I am wondering whether I could re-create the flames of Hell so that these flames would be waiting to

cause the souls of the dead, who have not willed and worshipped and prayed and purged themselves enough, to
suffer the everlasting pains that God so loved to inflict. The
truth is that all this time what I had in mind was a series of
desperate conjectures about how far it would be possible to
re-create the sun, the moon, the stars and this earth with all
their inhabitants exactly as they were in those days before
the death of God, I mean full of the fear of God and full of all
that Curtis Freshel was warning them about, helped by that
"Millennium Guild" in which Freshel's wife was so
absorbed. By saying "re-create" of course I don't mean
re-create the material substance of sun or moon or earth or
stars. I mean re-create the state of mind of the dwellers in
these worlds and you must remember that in the world-
dwellers I am not including animals and other non-human
creatures but only human beings and such entities as closely
resemble them. I don't suppose any of you three, Gor or
Maia or Cox, have ever seen a space-horse before. I expect
you think they are purely legendary apparitions. To tell you
the truth I had never seen one myself till I took possession of
this one body and soul.

'What I expect you three would like me most of all to tell
you is when and how I first met, during those early pere-
grinations with the Knights of King Arthur, the new Merlin
himself. I must be ready to tell you.' (So the Devil's
thoughts ran on.) 'But I don't feel like doing so just yet.
Why don't I? Well, I think it is because of that overpowering
sensation I had when I first saw him that he was part of
myself and I was part of him. Yes, it was no less than that.
Part of myself he was and part of himself I was. The second I
saw him that feeling came over me like the curling switch of
a whirlwind's tail. It was partly a feeling that something had
pulled me in half in order to make room for him. But it was
a still more extraordinary feeling that something had pulled
him in half in order to make room for me. Henceforth, I
thought to myself, Merlin is partly me and I am partly
Merlin. But soon after this a much more searching thought

leapt like a fish out of me and back again whence it had sprung. This thought said, "Never when I was within him or he was within me did I have the feeling of actually being Merlin to the extent of my thoughts being his thoughts. Never for a moment did I feel myself to be Merlin thinking to himself within me, though I certainly did feel myself to be me thinking to myself within Merlin. This surely shows that even with a Being possessed of the spiritual power of Merlin the old natural rules of identity, of me and thee, together with our thoughts, have to go on as usual." '

Well, the three adventurous explorers, Gor, Maia and Cox, not to speak of the Devil in the space-horse's body, went boldly on into the darkness. Little did any of them know that no less a being than Murdrawla, the largest of all the space-demons in existence, was hovering over them. The contact, a completely psychic one, between the Devil in possession of Cox's space-horse and Murdrawla was an extremely simple one, but not devoid of its own special dramatic interest. The Devil knew well that he was a good deal more powerful, as evil spirits go, than Murdrawla could claim to be, but he also knew that Murdrawla had not the slightest idea of this fact. To her mind, as soon as the impact between them began it was like a very powerful Air-Demon, namely herself, discovering the fact that some much smaller, almost infantile spirit of the same class had taken possession of Mr Cox's air-steed and was imposing its superior energy upon that creature's movements. It has always been Murdrawla's beauty that has fascinated visitors to space from sun and moon and earth and from every galaxy of stars. It is impossible to convey in ordinary human words the exquisite beauty of Murdrawla. How did space give birth to her? That was the question which it was impossible to prevent from coming into every visitor's mind. When David Cox asked the lady herself this daring question, her reply was as follows: 'I haven't, my dear sir, the faintest idea. I can remember when I was a child of two or three or four. I can remember when I was fourteen, but cannot remember any parents or any companion at any epoch. I'm very glad you like my looks. They are all I have.'

So Murdrawla floated above them and Gor was aware of the unequalled sweetness of the aura of feminine flesh. Maia was aware of it too, but being feminine herself it did not affect her in the same way though it affected her quite a lot. David Cox was extremely affected but what he felt was mingled with various other agitations. Gor was suffering from acute dyspepsia under his left rib as they all three moved on. Whatever it was, however, that hurt him under his right rib struck him now as being greatly eased. But the further and faster they went the worse did Gor's dyspeptic pain become till Maia couldn't help asking him why he was grabbing so desperately with both hands under his braces at the left top of his trousers. 'It's dyspepsia, my dear,' he replied. 'It's this old trouble I've had since I was fourteen at school.'

'It has nothing to do then with this naked angel or demon flying above our heads?'

'Oh no,' replied Gor decisively, 'nothing whatever. I had it before she appeared and I shall doubtless have it still when she has disappeared.'

'Perhaps,' said David Cox, 'if you prayed to the lady over our heads as if she were a goddess, she would act like a goddess and command that pain to go away. Pain is a thing, especially that kind of pain, that is particularly responsive to divine influence.'

'But how do I know,' cried Gor angrily, 'that this naked creature over our heads is a divine influence? How do I know that she isn't some pretty devilkin that God created for a special torment of the lost souls he loves gloating over in Hell?'

'Do you know what I think?' said Maia suddenly.

'Do tell us, for Heaven's sake!' cried Gor. 'What *you* think about this lady over our heads is the important thing. You are much more likely to grasp the situation than we are.'

At this point in their plight David Cox addressed Maia:

'What had we better do? You must understand this Being as none of us men can.'

'Well, I think she wants a lover. I think if you, Gor, or you, David Cox, were to stretch out your arms and throw them round her you would find she would yield at once to your embrace.'

'But would either of us be able to fly with her through space?'

'She would see to that,' responded Maia. 'An angel doesn't need help from a mortal man when she is holding him in her arms.'

It can be well imagined how the Devil, still in full possession of David Cox's space-horse, listened to this conversation. 'I wonder,' he thought within himself, 'what this space-angel would feel if, as David Cox embraced her, she suddenly became aware of my presence within the space-horse beneath them? It is really very queer how much better God understood me and I understood God than either of us has ever understood the thoughts of human beings or animals. I think I understand animals better than God does and he understands human beings, especially children, better than I do. Love and Hate are more interesting, far far more, than understanding. We don't need any understanding to love and hate. I long to ask this naked angel above us what she hates and what she loves, quite apart from me and God and men and women and children and animals and birds and insects. What I love most of all are shadows and what I hate most of all are ceilings. Why in the name of Heaven and Hell do we have to have those horrid, grey flat, colourless, meaningless, lifeless lids above the airy spaces of the room or rooms where our nicest human beings spend their lives? I, the Devil, have only to look at the backs of the books in this bookshelf in this room up the nine or eleven steps of this house, to see what I love best here: namely the backs of the four enormous folios of Littré's dictionary of the French language. But it is this lovely naked girl Murdrawla herself whom I would like most to obey at this juncture, if she would only speak up boldly and tell us all what would be the wisest thing for us to do.'

8

Gor felt an ecstasy of happiness when Murdrawla responded to his outstretched arms. In five minutes they were
locked together in a passionate embrace and for half a year
they were flying and floating sometimes between Cox and
Maia, sometimes alone in the darkness without the sight of
a single star. Their excrement, like that of a pair of en-
amoured horses or cattle slid down through the darkness,
followed by their urine; and as wandering pedestrians in
London's most frequented parks saw it, or even perhaps felt
it fall, rumours kept spreading that certain swiftly moving
vessels were careless about their sanitary overflow. As can
be imagined, the Devil in his exultant possession of the soul
— and in a sense of the body too — of David Cox's space-
horse found himself perpetually conveying that highly-
strung adventurer into positions from which he could spy
with not very honourable interest upon the united and
double-enhanced swooping of the love-wave whose foam-
white vibrations made the air quiver as it carried Gor's
caressing ardours and Murdrawla's aerial responses within
the mystic dance-curve of zodiacal destiny. But Cox's rap-
turous contemplations of aerial love, accompanied by
Maia's virginal commentaries, were not the only background to what Gor and Murdrawla were enjoying. It was
the Devil who had suddenly got into his inexhaustible head
a new idea. He had begun to feel that his guidance of the
space-horse that was pulling Cox along was not causing as

much disturbance to the three friends, Gor, Cox and Maia, as he had intended to cause. It had had, as was only too clear to him now, no effect at all upon the movements of Murdrawla. Then it suddenly came into his head that he must do something to vex, hinder, trouble, disturb, interrupt, delay, defeat, agitate, upset, bewilder, confuse, harass, invalidate the love between Gor and Murdrawla. What could he do? They were so happy together, so absolutely absorbed in each other. What could he do to shake up and belittle their frantic and abandoned emotion? Then the idea occurred to him. Yes! Yes! That is what he would do! No sooner had it come into his head than he did it. He shook off his hold on Cox's space-horse and left it free to follow its own will. Then he quietly, cunningly, silently, surreptitiously, left Cox and Maia to themselves and flung his whole personality and all his strength into the stick Gor held in his hand, which contact with the naked girl had not loosened from his grip. Oh how happy the Devil felt when he had plunged into Gor's stick and taken full possession of it! Gor did not relax for a second his embrace of Murdrawla because of the stick in his hand. If he clutched the stick tighter because — though he knew it not — the Devil was in it, he embraced Murdrawla closer than before. But the Devil was thinking exultantly within himself: 'What is now to prevent me from ruling the whole universe? Riding as I am upon the bodies — even between the bodies now and then — of these two lovers and dominating with absolute control this magic stick of Gor, and knowing, as few others in the world do, that God is dead, who is there that can prevent my declaring myself Lord of the entire universe?'

'My space-horse is acting very queerly,' said Cox to Maia. 'I can't understand what has come over it.'

'I expect,' said Maia to Cox, 'it has to do with those two making love as they float above our heads. When human beings act in an unusual way, some way they're not accustomed to witness, animals always tend to get funny.'

'I wish,' said Cox to Maia, 'I hadn't started making love

to Murdrawla. If only I'd just let her sail over me untouched all would have been well.'

'All *is* well,' said Maia to Cox.

'I pray so,' said Cox to Maia.

'I wish we could put a stop,' said Maia to Cox, 'to this love-making in the air. I think it is not only terribly agitating to your space-horse but I begin to find it rather bad for my health. I have never before felt seasick in this space-trip of ours but I have felt like that twice lately now. And I've been flying quite as calmly as usual. I'm sure it's the effect upon me of this airy-fairy love-making.'

While Gor and Murdrawla followed by Cox and Maia were steadily encircling the sun, the moon and the stars, led by Gor's stick, which in its convulsive possession by the Devil was able to be instinctively aware how closely Cox and Maia were following it, the Arch-Eagle of the Universe in a remote portion of space was unfolding its tremendous wings. Its parents had instructed it, when it first emerged from its colossal egg-shell which it broke into tiny bits, how to unfold its wings so as not to create too much disturbance in the air. But it was not long after it had learnt this lesson, that they and their nest had disappeared forever. When its gigantic wings were at last unfolded the Arch-Eagle gazed intently towards the sun, moon, earth and stars and did not fail to notice Murdrawla and her lover Gor with his Devil-possessed stick, followed by Maia and Cox. Maia was moving through the air just as gracefully as if she were flying and Cox was rather irritably trying to drive his space-horse in the direction of a deliberate circle round sun, moon, earth and stars. No sooner had the Arch-Eagle caught sight of this group than he began flying towards them. There was something about the couple of lovers who led them that especially appealed to him. Before his parents had disappeared forever into the Heaven of space-dwellers they had named their son Paragon; so it was Paragon who came rushing down and tried to seize Murdrawla by the throat. The sweetness of her body was such, however, and her laugh when she felt him there so enthralling that his jaws refused to close, especially as his head was receiving extremely sharp blows from a stick that Gor carried. The next thing that happened was simple and natural enough. Paragon unclosed his jaws, unfolded his great wings and rose up above them all, where he kept flying backwards and forwards just as Murdrawla and Gor had done before. Maia, with nothing but her arms and legs, and Cox with his erratic space-horse, felt extremely uneasy as they watched this huge bird, that looked more and more like a dragon as it grew darker, flying backwards and forwards above their heads.

But Paragon's mind was working actively. 'What can I do with them?' he thought to himself, 'now that I have got this little group under my control? Heaven and Earth! I believe I've got it. Why shouldn't I convey them all to that remote and solitary region of empty space of which I caught a glimpse a week ago? I might establish a little kingdom for them there! I think this fellow Gor and this exquisitely lovely creature Murdrawla would make a fine king and queen. In fact I might go further and have their kingdom turned into a sort of psychic empire over every country in the world. I could fly to all these countries and carry with me a paper for them to sign submitting to the spiritual authority, whether they are Christians or Buddhists or Mohammedans, of King Gor and his great mysterious wife Queen Murdrawla.'

The great Arch-Eagle Paragon, according to what he had decided, now spread his enormous wings, and using them with the comfortable and easy motion of a tidal wave whose original earthquake was far away, swept Gor and Murdrawla and David Cox with his hard-working space-horse and the gallant solitary Maia flying quite alone, without causing them any special agitation, till, somewhere about eleven o'clock in the morning by Abertackle time he established them safely in the secluded region he had discovered. Once there it was easy for him to inspire them, for the Arch-Eagle had more psychic power than any other offspring of pure space, with all the daring and audacity he had been formulating for them in his own mind. He soon collected them all around him and one of the most re-markable conferences began that have ever taken place in the world. Perhaps it was the most remarkable of all. At any rate it shall now be described. The first word to be uttered came from the hooked beak of the Arch-Eagle; and it took the form of a simple and direct question. It was addressed by the Arch-Eagle to the Devil who suddenly emerged from Gor's stick and presented himself, horns and all, in his accustomed human shape, at the head of the bed of cloudy mist upon which, side by side, Gor and Murdrawla were seated.

'Who are you?' said Paragon to the Devil.

'Well,' replied the latter, 'I am tempted to reply "Ask Mister Cox", for he belongs, as indeed does Mr Gor also, to the race of earth-dwellers who invented me. They also were the ones who invented God, although I shrewdly suspect that if you had put your question to God before he died of old age, he would have retorted that he invented himself. Yes, both God and the Devil were the invention of the earth dwellers, God being their idea of the first cause of every-thing Good and the Devil being their idea of the first cause of everything Evil. The human race in its earliest ages must have had a wild and desperate fear of all animals with horns, which must be the reason that, though they imagined my form and shape to be human, they always visualized me with horns protruding from my head.'

'What did you feel like when you were first invented by the Christians? For we all know that neither the Buddhists nor the Mohammedans believe in you.'

'Well,' replied the Devil with the greatest ease. 'I just felt an enormous sense of relief. You see they invented me to embody all the most wicked things they felt themselves and I can't tell you what relief I felt when I found that to please the people who invented me *and to be* their invention to the limit, I had only to hate as much as I could! Oh how I loved hating! And to hate as much as I liked and could — Oh what a perfect joy!'

While the Devil was recovering his breath after his eulogy upon hatred Gor was examining his stick very carefully, the stick out of which the Devil had burst forth. 'How did this Evil one,' he enquired of Murdrawla, hugging her to his heart, 'get out of my stick as it lay between us?'

'The question I would like to answer, if only I could,' replied Murdrawla, 'is how he got into it. I have the idea, though how that came into my head I don't know, that before he got into your stick he was in possession of David Cox's space-horse. But if that were so it seems very queer that he should leave possession of a horse to enter a stick.'

'I expect you can never tell with devils; I expect they never know themselves,' said Gor, 'what they're going to do next.'

'Well,' said Maia, 'we must think clearly and decide definitely what we're going to do. Our present lord and master is our friend Paragon the Arch-Eagle who brought us hither. I suggest that humbly and naturally, without pretending any emotion we don't feel, we ask him what he would advise us to do.'

'I can reply to that at once,' said the Arch-Eagle. 'I advise you all to agree simultaneously, without electing or voting or arguing or discussing the matter at all, to make Gor your King and Murdrawla your Queen and appoint Maia as your Defence Minister and David Cox as your Finance Minister. Then I would, all four of you together, with what help I can give you, draw up a document, in as legal language as you know how, announcing that we have established in this region of empty space a new world kingdom above all Christians, all Buddhists, all Mohammedans, yes! a psychic, or spiritual World-Kingdom, entitled "The Kingdom of Mankind". I myself, Paragon, the super Arch-Eagle, will be the herald or royal messenger of this new state, and I will fly to every country in the world carrying our legal paper and I will make the government of each country I visit sign with its official signatures its spiritual adherence and submission to our universal world rule.'

Gor and Murdrawla calmly accepted their position as King and Queen of *Mankind's Kingdom*, of which Maia became the Minister of Defence and Cox the Minister of Finance, while the Arch–Eagle, whose name was Paragon, became the courier or herald of the New State. The Arch–Eagle had no difficulty in securing General de Gaulle's signature nor that of Dr Adenauer but he was refused any by East Germany and also by South Africa because of apartheid, and also by Turkey and Pakistan. New Zealand and Australia took a long time to persuade and Canada would have been the same, if it had not been that using a wise hint from a subtle writer in that remarkable country the Arch–Eagle flew through the office window of one of their chief foreign correspondents when he was fast asleep, and obtained his signature while he was in one of the curious nightmares his sleep was subject to, a nightmare which lent itself to the Arch–Eagle's appearance and request.

Then it happened that from a part of America where there was a settlement of Red Indians without one white man, or one black man, or even — for it was at some distance from China — one yellow man, there came an appeal to the great-winged Emissary of this New State of Mankind to pause and allow them to consider the object of his journey. With every degree of willingness, as you can imagine, the Arch–Eagle stopped in his flight, and entered into a colloquy with the Red Indians and their Chief which ended in the signature by this latter, in a handwriting that made King Gor and Queen Murdrawla feel exultant when they saw it, of a special request to be included among those who supported the New State of Mankind.

But what none of the supporters of the New State realized, and what even the messenger of the New State didn't realize, was that before the time of Adam and Eve, that is to say before our human race began its career upon earth, there existed a Being whom all the living creatures of our world, fish, animals, birds, reptiles, when they referred to him in any intercourse among themselves — and this included insects also — always referred to as the 'Unknown One'.

This Being had the body of an enormous lizard and the head of a rhinoceros; but out of its eyes there looked forth an expression that was most decidedly human, and in addition to this there emerged from its shoulders two rather short but otherwise quite normal arms and hands. This Being lived in a large cave on the outskirts of the region that had now become known through the activity of the Arch-Eagle as the New State of Mankind. Among the characters of this New State who have now become familiar to us, it was naturally the Devil who was the most active; and it was the Devil who was the first among them all to have the audacity to visit the Unknown One in his cave.

So inured was the Devil, by reason of his various experiences under the authority of God, to pain, that he felt as if there was nothing particularly queer or unusual when, having boldly entered his cave, he found the Unknown One wriggling and scriggling and clutching with his short arms and shorter hands at everything within reach of the bed of straw upon which he or it lay extended.

'You are suffering, Master?'

'Who in the name of God are you?'

'My usual name is the Devil, but in my time I've had grander names than that.'

'How did you know I was in pain?'

'If anyone in the world knows what pain is like and what it makes one to do it is I.'

'How is that?' enquired the Unknown One.

'Because God,' responded the other, quietly seating himself on the floor of the cave and folding his arms round his shins, 'employed me for hundreds of years in the task of increasing the pain of his enemies by pushing them back into the flames out of which they had managed to scramble.

That, as you probably know, Unknown One, was God's chief pleasure. Paul, who invented Christianity, was the letter-writing missionary. But where he muddled things up a bit was in regard to Love and Hate. He learned in watching the exquisite delight that God took in torturing his enemies and making them believe that the flames that were causing them such pain would last for ever what Hate was. He knew that such men as the Marquis de Sade and Gilles de Retz have always been examples of wickedness, whereas God's delight in burning his enemies has become something like a Law of Nature that fits in perfectly with his Love for those among us who try to love him. How did Paul muddle things up so? I know he lived long before the Marquis de Sade and Gilles de Retz. But that wasn't the reason. The reason was that in his own heart — and I know I'm right there — Paul felt Love and Hate contending and sometimes one and sometimes the other dominating him completely. But the point, oh Unknown One, suffering such pain, is simply and solely the nature of pain! It certainly is a queer thing. Compare it with its opposite, for example. Yes! Compare it with pleasure. When we enjoy pleasure we feel it all around us. It is in everything we look at with our eyes, hear with our ears, smell, feel, taste! But this confounded pain that St Paul delights to see his God of Love inflict on those who hate him, is not all around us, is not in our eyes, ears, taste and smell. Pain is always localized, whereas pleasure is spread abroad in all directions. When the adorable Saint appears who has made us happy we look round us on all sides, we dance and play and sing. But when the stern punisher of us for our sins and wrongdoings turns up do we look round? Not a bit of it! We clutch with our hands just as you are doing now that particular place in our suffering body where the pain is lodged.'

'Please go away,' said the Unknown One to the Devil, and the Devil obeyed him. He flew as quickly as he could to their little encampment and related to them all that he had found. The Unknown One, he explained to them, 'is suf-

fering from some internal pain. He squirms and shivers and
shudders and he keeps clutching with his hands, which are
just like ours, only his arms are much shorter than ours, at
every curve or protuberance in his body from where his legs
begin to where his neck begins. At last, after I had been
talking to him for a little while about the difference between
pain and pleasure, he asked me to go away; and I obeyed
him without protest. I wonder what is the matter with him
and whether it's anything serious?'

'What is he like,' enquired Murdrawla, 'apart from his
legs and hands?'

The Devil pondered for a minute. 'What I think he's like,'
he said, 'is one of those monsters we read about and see
pictures of in books. I expect he *is* one of those monsters
who has lived in this cave ever since those early days and by
long experience knows exactly where to find a flock of
sheep or a group of cattle from which he can carry a good
meal for himself back to his cave. I sat on the floor while I
talked to him, but he had a bed of very soft and comfortable
hay which long experience must have taught him how to
collect and arrange. Unless my imagination is completely
running away with me, it struck me more than once as I sat
on the floor clinging to the top of my socks, that it was
crossing the mind of the Unknown One whether it was
worth his while to seize me with one of his human hands
and short human arms and devour me, beginning with my
head and ending with my feet.

'Is he like any animal alive today?' enquired Gor.

'Well,' replied the Devil, 'he is a little like a rhinoceros. If
some magician were to turn him into a beast I am sure that
would be the one into which he'd be transformed. But at the
same time,' the Devil went on, 'there is something about
him that makes you think of some sort of enormous shark.
Is there such a thing, do any of you know of such a thing, as
a shark almost as big as a whale?'

There was quite a stir in the little camp of the New State
of Mankind when the Devil asked this question. The liquid

voice of Maia and the gravelly voice of David Cox collided together as they both answered. 'Oh yes,' cried Maia. 'I've seen pictures of a creature exactly like what you describe. I'm sure that in the depths of the ocean there are monsters exactly like that!'

'Oh but you don't have to go to the bottom of the ocean,' cried David Cox, 'to find such things! They come out of the sea, and swim up the estuaries to the rivers! My own home at Abertackle where I was born looked out on an estuary where fishermen used to drag up in their great nets the most extraordinary creatures. Yes, I have seen them take out of their nets and kill things just like the monster whose cave you've been into!'

It was the voice of Murdrawla that finally floated over all their heads, like a gentle zephyr above a lake of thick-headed wrangling reeds.

'We must act as our wise Devil did,' murmured Murdrawla, 'and sit on the floor of the World while the rising tide of Nature's wildest intention is checked by a splutter of chance and calmed down by the steadily blowing wind of destiny.'

9

The present camp of the New State of Mankind was soon sunk in deep slumber. Gor and Murdrawla slept in each other's arms. Maia slept alone with her head on a pillow of her own making which she had propped up against the stump of a tree which had been blown down long ago. David Cox slept not far from Maia with his head upon a very large and richly embroidered pillow which Maia had made especially for him. By eight o'clock that night the Devil arose from a comfortable sleep he had allowed himself to enjoy inside the entrance to an old badger's hole only a few yards distant from the two heads of Gor and Murdrawla as they lay side by side. The Devil had no sooner emerged from his badger's hole than he decided he had been unwise in allowing himself even that retreat. 'I bet my life,' he told himself, 'that Old Horror has already come across from his cave and is exploring our camp, hoping to find we've forgotten some child or some cat or dog or serving-maid whom he could snatch up and carry home to devour mouthful by mouthful at his confounded pleasure.'

The Devil had hardly experienced the wafture of this disturbing thought pass through him like the whiff-whiff-whiff of the breath of an infantile volcano when he saw in the distance the unmistakable figure of the Unknown One lumbering heavily towards him. Down on his stomach he went, and sprawling along by the aid of tufts of grass and withered stalks of bracken he worked himself clear of his retreat till he reached the feet of Gor and Murdrawla, round whom he scrabbled as softly as he could and then sat up hugging his knees as he had done on the monster's floor and watched for his approach. 'Ought I,' the Devil said to himself, 'to wake these people of the New State of Mankind? At this moment it might mean a wild scuffle between them and the Unknown One which would end in his victory and not theirs. I feel entirely on the side of these people, though why I have such a normal, earthly feeling I don't know. Gor and Cox would take it for granted that being the Devil and not God I should be on the Unknown One's side; but I fancy Maia would understand things better. She, with a wise woman's instinct, would know that in all those hell-burnings I was God's agent and servant because of my cowardice and of my fear that if I didn't obey him he would toss me into the flames and begin at once whispering in my ear his gloating delight in torture — "not for only a million years but forever and forever and forever will you burn in these flames." No,' thought the Devil. 'It would be a mistake to wake them all now; not only because it would give the monster an opportunity to leap upon them or whatever thing belonging to them he pleased; for if they were suddenly aroused from sleep they would all be too confused to defend themselves properly.'

'Thinking thus,' as Homer always says, the Devil remained in his seated position watching most intently the approach of the monster. 'If he comes straight here,' thought the Devil, 'he'll see that I am not asleep, but on the other hand if I lie on my back and pretend to be asleep he may leap upon me and make me his victim, which is the last thing I want to happen.'

What he did accordingly, after thinking thus, was to work himself or worm himself backwards till he was well behind the feet of Gor and Murdrawla. Here he remained on his back, but not deprived of the power to peep out over the feet of Gor and Murdrawla and watch the advancing Unknown One.

It was then that out of the badger's hole at the entrance to which our friend had paused ere making his former discoveries there emerged an extremely youthful badger. This apparition was observed at once by the Unknown One who came, leap after leap, towards it. The small badger, however, clearly had all its wits about it, for it slyly waited till the monster was quite near and then with a leap worthy of any offspring of the monster itself, rushed round him and scampered off in the direction from which they had all come. The monster followed him as well as it could; but it was evident that the fact that they had all come from the direction in which the badger fled made its pursuit much more difficult. 'I suppose,' said the Devil to himself, 'the scent of such a move as we all made to get here has made it very hard to pursue any one of us along the route we took to reach this place unless kept in sight.'

The monster was certainly quite out-run by the little badger when this small animal emerged from the deep hole made by its ancestors thousands of years ago; and as the Devil watched, the Unknown One returned in an evidently exhausted state towards its Cave.

It was then that an exciting idea came into the Devil's mind. 'Why,' he thought, 'don't I build for myself out of these tree logs and tree stumps and fallen branches a very strong but very small woodman's hut? And why don't I keep in it little toy figures which I could easily carve out of wood and paint them so that they would represent all the human beings that have lived in the world before the New State of Mankind was constructed. Yes, I would paint Red Indians and Black Africans and White Settlers and Yellow Chinamen. I would have black and white and red and yellow little men, all in a row on a shelf. Then if any children came — Oh!' and the Devil heaved such a deep sigh! 'What would I not give for some grandchildren! Just two! Only two! One boy and one girl!'

The word grandchildren, for an innate reason in his own mind caught the ear of Gor who gave Murdrawla a special hug and sat up. 'How could I have grandchildren,' he asked the Devil, 'if I haven't a son or daughter?'

'By adoption,' replied the Devil. 'That is how I'm thinking of having mine!'

Still waiting rather eagerly to follow to the end the topic of grandchildren, the Devil shrugged off the dramatic finale of the Unknown One's pursuit of the little badger, a finale which must have left the monster groaning with pain on his bed and the little creature slipping with delicious satisfaction down the larder-drop of his ancestors' subterranean dwelling.

But Gor had awakened Murdrawla, who found the Devil regarding her with an expression of worshipful devotion, for if there were anyone better acquainted with the best way to appreciate myth-creating ladies such an one had never as yet come near Murdrawla.

The shameless, plain-speaking David Cox was also awake now and what he said brought another aspect of their journey to their minds. 'We'd better have a drink and go to sleep again, for the early morning is the best time to reach the centre of any space journey.'

Maia's was the last word. 'None of us know what any of us feel. So "on all together!" is the word: and let the future keep its revelation.'

As soon as the Unknown One had gone galumphing back to his cave and the Devil knew that Gor and Murdrawla and David Cox and Maia were all awake, he got up and followed the monster. It can be believed how staggered he was when on entering he found there were two of them in the cave. The monster knew him at once and introduced him to the other monster whom he described as his mother and whose name, he said, was Wow. 'No,' he went on, 'Wow darling, we can't gobble him up, because he's got a much more powerful spirit than we have and a much more powerful spirit than any human beings on this Earth excepting only Red Indians, who, as you used to teach me when I was little, were able without any weapons at all but simply by the power of the spirit to dominate every other race in the world. This personage, featured and embodied like a man — like a little man — but with horns coming out of his head, has some connection with that Being who called himself "Father of All" and whom the Earthlings called God. He will explain to you, Wow darling, what the connection exactly was. I have forgotten. But he will tell you himself.'

The Unknown One was right. The Devil had no sooner been introduced to Wow, whose hand he kissed devoutly, than he began delivering the sort of regular lecture on the theological, psychological and biblical revelation between God and himself, such as anyone as yet unschooled in the appropriate expressions would have wanted to hear.

'But how could you,' enquired old Madame Wow, whose appearance because of her age tended to accentuate the ferocity of her face, 'bear to obey such a cruel burner of his enemies as I have always heard your God was?'

'Well, lady,' replied the Devil, 'if I hadn't thrown back again into the flames any human soul who was scrambling out, God would have pitched me in at once. It was extraordinary the pleasure God derived from causing pain. I was present at the confession of Gilles de Retz or Bluebeard as they called him and his fear of falling into God's flames certainly made God a crueller Being than any Bluebeard.'

'Thank you very much indeed, Mr Devil, for all you've told me. I shall never forget it.'

Wow's words were uttered in such a sincere voice that the Devil could not help accepting them as absolute truth. 'May I,' he asked her nervously, 'beg you to tell me one simple thing.'

'By all means,' replied Wow, and the Devil felt highly delighted that he had reached a point of intimacy as deep as this. 'How long,' he asked her, 'has your race dominated this particular position in space?'

'Only a little over two thousand years,' replied Wow. 'I can tell you that with exact certitude, because it was from

you earthlings that we have learnt the art of numeration;
and we have kept it up very carefully, and we possess an
exquisitely delicate calendar, if such you could call it, giving
all the signatures of our forbears — not of course their
pictures, for as you know none of us look very pretty —
going back year after year, century after century; just as if
we were not monsters at all but very learned and scientific
historians.'

10

'I am very much impressed by all you say, Lady Wow. Oh yes, Lady Wow, I am deeply impressed by the idea of your ancestors in this cave for over two thousand years having kept a commemoration and calendar of all the centuries as they passed, for my own life has had nothing, no! has never had anything, with which to celebrate its uneven course, and I have always longed for something of the kind.'

'May I follow your example, Monsieur Devil, and ask you a bold question?' enquired Wow.

'O please do!' cried the Devil. 'I shall be so thrilled to try and answer it if I can.'

'Did this cruel God of the earthlings,' Wow asked him, 'create you? Or, if not, who or what did? Or did you perhaps have horned parents like yourself who brought you into this world?'

'You have asked me,' replied the Devil, 'the most important question in the world; and I will try to answer it. Your question is, "How did the cruel God of the Christians flattered by St Paul as being the God of Love and how did his *supposed opposite*, namely myself, the Devil, come to exist? Who, or what, created them?" '

The Devil spoke with such earnestness that both the monster, or the Unknown One, and his mother Wow, listened intently to every syllable.

'It was the human spirit that created both God and me,' said the Devil. 'Human nature contained in itself something beyond what Nature alone — I mean the elements of air and water and earth and fire — could provide. This something was, and undoubtedly still is, the *Power to Create*. This power comes from the human spirit containing in itself all that it calls Good and all that it calls Evil. It applies those adjectives of course to everything it knows of; every projection of mind, every projection of matter, in the entire universe, or if you prefer that idea, in the entire multiverse, was quickly endowed, the moment the human race appeared, with its own notion of what was good and what was evil. How was it, then, you may ask, that their Christian God who ought to have been, and indeed was, according to St Paul, who by his crafty use of the scattered words of Jesus Christ may be said to have invented Christianity, a Being composed of Love, was soon understood to be a monster of cruelty who gloated over the sufferings of people's souls in Hell, and as he hovered over them there delighted in reminding them that their pain was not for a million years but for ever and for ever and for ever, and that it had come to them because they were his enemies. But, as various human atheists have argued, who wouldn't, what decent man or woman wouldn't, call a cruel monster like the God of Christianity their enemy? What did Jesus himself cry out when he was on the Cross? "Eloi! Eloi! lama sabachthani?" "My God, my God, why hast thou forsaken me?" To this the Jesus-lovers who are atheists ought to answer: "He deserted you, oh Best of Men, for the simple reason that he had fooled you from the start in making you believe that he existed." '

It was at that point in their conversation that the Devil heard a sound in the air outside the cave, a sound that by this time he had come to know very well indeed. It was none other than their ally, Paragon, the Arch-Eagle. 'Oh,' thought the Devil, 'if only I could lure one or other of them — perhaps both! — out of the cave's entrance! Maybe if I told him they were our enemies — now that he seems to have become quite definitely our friend and our helper — he would swallow the Unknown One or the Unknown One's Mother, at a gulp, and I'd be spared any further explanation of how our silly earthlings egged on by St Paul and his passion for a deity composed of Love just as — you know the sort of thing — is composed of oil. Oh how I long to hear the wings of Paragon at this moment! Yes, monster, you would have reason for shuddering then! Yes, Madame Wow, you would have reason for crying out "Wow! Wow! Wow! Wow!" if I had heard those great wings and had lured you out of your cave! I wonder what happens in the inside of our Arch-Eagle when a creature as big as the Unknown One or as big as the Unknown One's mummy gurgles down into a place like our Arch-Angelic eagle's belly? Will it struggle to come up again? And if so what will happen? Oh Arch-Eagle, descend and help us!'

The Devil issued from the Cave with prayers to the Arch-Eagle Paragon. But the last thing he expected or the last thing he could have thought of expecting was, as is so often the case with human beings as well as with gods and devils, the thing that now happened. The magic all-conquering sword of King Arthur, torn from his hand in the last battle of his life, the battle of Lyonesse, came suddenly floating up from the Earth through the avenue of space which Gor and Murdrawla and Maia and David Cox had followed. There it was! There was Excalibur itself within reach of the Devil's hand! The Devil seized it. The Devil brandished it. 'Just think!' he thought to himself, 'after all *it's* gone through, and after all I've gone through, that this should happen! Oh how I wish God hadn't died a natural death! How heavenly it would have been if I could have killed him with Excalibur!' He looked round. No, he had come out of the cave alone. No sign of mummy Wow or of her offspring the monster.

'Oh what can I do with Excalibur?' cried the Devil to himself: and then, with rather a pathetic gesture when you come to think of it, he raised his left hand — not the one which was brandishing Excalibur — to his forehead as if to make sure that his horns were there, in other words to make sure that by brandishing Excalibur he hadn't changed from being himself. 'The truth is,' he said to himself, 'my contact with these earthlings, combined with their space-born Murdrawla, has had a queer effect upon my mind.'

Very slowly the Devil, having reassured himself about his horns being in their usual place, walked out of the cave. He was just going to direct his steps to where he had left Gor and Murdrawla when a sound he had never heard before came to his ears. It came from up the slope towards the base of the Moelwyn Range and when the Devil looked in that direction he saw a person walking. It looked like a human dwarf with a monstrously large face and long legs and arms. The Devil hurried boldly towards it.

'Who are you?' said the person to him. 'You look just like all the stories I used to hear as a child about the Devil.'

'I am the Devil,' was our friend's answer. 'May I enquire who you are?'

'Well, at any rate we both speak the same language. We have both lived on the Earth,' said the person. 'My name is Gonflab,' he went on. 'As you can see, my arms and legs come straight out of my head. What on earth is called a stomach is in the back portion of my head. I bite and chew and masticate with my mouth and teeth. I have no neck or shoulders, no chest, no belly . . . nothing but arms and legs.'

The Devil looked Gonflab over and over with the greatest interest. Yes, he had spoken quite correctly. His head went back absurdly. Its back was a lot bigger than its front. Yes! He had no stomach, no neck, no chest, no ribs, no belly. His legs and arms came straight out of his head. 'How do you kill for your food, Gonflab?' the Devil asked him.

'You will see, Mr Devil, how the Creator of the World has only recently died leaving his creation to look after itself, or Nature to look after herself, and if you examine my hands you will also see how it has been arranged that I can kill what I want to eat.' Thus speaking, Gonflab held his right hand close beneath the Devil's face, who examined it carefully as he had been told to do. He noticed that it had tremendously long and curved and sharp nails.

'What do you find, Gonflab, in this space-world to eat?'

'There are lots of things, Mr Devil, that suit me perfectly,' Gonflab replied. 'Whether,' he went on, 'you have ever noticed these space-bats which fly about in pairs holding tightly to each other I don't know; but they make extremely tasty food.'

'No, I've never seen —' the Devil began — and then he chanced to catch sight of a pair of the very creatures they were talking about and he saw Gonflab seize them with both his hands and squeeze them, prodding them as he did so through and through with his sharp nails, into his widely open mouth.

'I wonder,' the Devil asked himself as he watched this going on, 'whether by clinging together the bats make their death easier, or whether by quickening their flight in that way they make it harder to catch them?'

And then it was that the Devil's mind swung over to quite a different cogitation. 'Suppose,' he thought, 'our great friendly Arch-Eagle Paragon was to come hovering above our heads at this moment, would he, could he, might he, seize upon Gonflab himself by the head and with his super-aquiline claws tear his head open and swallow everything in it and then begin making a feast for himself out of Gonflab's two sturdy legs after he had bitten off both his arms and watched them sink side by side down towards the world that had so many similar bones covered with sweet flesh. Paragon's appetite,' the Devil told himself, 'will be greatly excited by the taste of the flesh upon Gonflab's leg-bones, not to think of what it gets out of the back of Gonflab's head.' Tightly the Devil's right fist clutched the handle of Excalibur. 'Just think of my having King Arthur's sword!' his whole soul cried within itself.

The Devil had no sooner come leaping down after disposing of Gonflab, his left hand repeatedly and almost mechanically touching his own horns, to make sure he was still his proper self, and his right hand clutching the handle of King Arthur's Excalibur than he became aware that both the monster's mother Wow and the monster — otherwise the Unknown One — were cautiously, cunningly, craftily, calculatingly, encompassing mankind's new camp with steps as camouflaged as if each paw they put down was touching velvet. 'Where can Paragon the Arch-Eagle be? There he is! Oh thanks be! He must have seen that I was clutching Arthur's Excalibur, for the moment he descended he seized upon Wow, the Unknown One's mother, and held her by the top of her head. He then actually turned his arch-angelic eyes on me as much as to say, "I see you've got Excalibur, so I know what you will do." I did what he hinted in a moment. With one sweep of the sword I cut off Wow's head. Down, down, down, down it sank and the people of Abertackle must have seen it falling, for the touch of Excalibur threw a magic light on it and it must have looked like a meteorite as it fell. You can believe how I, the Devil, pressed my left hand against my horns to be sure I was in my right senses; and then brandishing Excalibur rushed after the monster.'

That there was indeed every reason for him to pursue the Unknown One or the monster, having with the help of the arch-eagle disposed for ever of this being's mother, Wow, who had been quite as deadly a creature, if not more so, than her terrific son, the Devil knew as his left hand flew to his horns to make sure he was still himself, and he now clasped the handle of King Arthur's Excalibur very tightly and pondered in his mind whether he had better cut at the monster's throat as he had done with Wow or stab him to the heart. 'Is his heart in the same place in his body as ours is?' he said to himself. But suddenly a totally different idea came into his head. He asked himself whether it would not be more exciting and more full of strange possibilities if he made the monster a prisoner and kept him in bonds, but always in such a way that at any moment he could be released, like a fierce chained-up dog, and sent rushing at someone whom it was desirable to attack. But the Devil didn't quell this sudden inspiration at this point. He let it carry him, he encouraged it to carry him, as far as it wanted to go. And it evidently wanted to go a long distance. What he now began thinking about was the idea of binding together with a huge rope the whole camp of his friends, these human explorers of space, Gor with Murdrawla, Cox with his horse, Maia with all her mystical insight, and then calling upon the Arch-Eagle to spread its wings and grasp the rope with its beak and to carry them on and on and on and on and on into empty space, to let happen what would.

The Devil's inspiration worked out well. The Arch-Eagle was delighted with the idea. The thought of being in the position of carrying space-ward beyond all known worlds this whole camp of human civilization was just the kind of thought to appeal to him.

The first event to happen in connection with the Devil's activity before the Arch-Eagle carried him, clinging to Cox's horse, beyond all known worlds, was his killing of the Unknown One. He hid himself so skilfully behind Cox's horse that when the monster came near it gave him his opportunity. Then he rushed out and with his right hand tightening its grip upon Arthur's Excalibur he plunged its whole length, clear up to the hilt, through the monster's heart, and, as the Arch-Eagle carried the Devil up with the rest, the Devil could see the monster he had slain and Excalibur gleaming out of its body, sinking down, just as the monster's mother Wow had sunk, into the world of sun and moon and earth and stars.

After watching the descent of the monster, otherwise 'the Unknown One', with Excalibur through his heart, the Devil asked himself whether he had better cling to a strip of Murdrawla's night-shirt which Gor's impassioned embrace had loosened and which flew trailing through the air, or whether he'd better hang on to a strip of wood which projected downwards from the rear of Cox's wagon? Or finally whether it wouldn't be wisest of all to clutch the hem of Maia's skirt, seeing that the weight of all her garments was supported and held up by a beautifully strong broad belt which she had fastened carefully and securely round her waist. He finally decided in favour of the strip of Murdrawla's night-gown, for he recalled well how the first they had all seen of her was her form as she floated in that night-gown across and across the ascending space-path of the upward flight of them all.

11

Up, up, up they all went, until day after day and night after night passed over their heads for what struck them as a time too long to be measured by any human calculation.

At length they began murmuring among themselves. 'I don't believe we are going up into space any more,' murmured Gor.

'I think the darkness round us now reminds me of what it felt like at home before midnight was chimed from the church tower,' murmured Cox.

'I thought a moment ago,' murmured Maia, 'that I heard those chimes.' It was then that Gor suddenly remembered his sister Nelly who had been so fond of him and of whom he hadn't had a thought for what seemed like hundreds of years. 'Goodbye to you all,' whispered Murdrawla, escaping from Gor's arms and gliding off till she was out of sight. 'I can smell the seaweeds of Go,' announced Gor. 'We shall go down near the shore.'

'Abertackle!' they all murmured with one voice. 'We are home.'

Cataclysm

1

In the little town of Riddle in the county of Squat in the west
of Bumbledom there was a young man called Yok. He had
just reached his seventeenth birthday on the first of January
in the year nineteen-hundred and sixty, and he now sat by
his open hearth on which burned a glowing red fire. Yok
was his Christian name. His surname was Pok. Opposite
him on the other side of the fire in a less comfortable chair
sat his sister Quo Pok, who was still sixteen.

'I have decided at last that I'll do it,' said Yok Pok. 'I've
been thinking about it very carefully from every possible
angle, for more than a couple of years; and I have now
decided that I'll do it.'

Miss Quo looked at him with alarm. All manner of wild
thoughts rushed through her mind. Was her brother
thinking of suicide? Was he thinking of killing them both?
Was he thinking of leaving their home and setting off to
visit Paris or Berlin or Jerusalem? And if so, was he thinking
of taking her with him? She had longed dreamed of seeing
something of the great world before she grew too old to
travel. But there was a look in her brother's face that scared
her. What in heaven's name had he decided to do? Then
without further delay he told her. 'I have decided,' he said
quietly, 'to destroy the whole human race.'

Miss Quo gasped and stared intently at him. Had her
brother gone mad? She suddenly remembered that her
mother had once told her that her great-great-grandfather

had been put into a lunatic asylum, where he had been kept until he died. Could it be — no, surely, surely not — that the grave, earnest face, looking so intently at her, was that of a madman? 'But tell me, Yok, Oh for pity's sake tell me what you mean by saying such a thing? Destroy the human race? But you and I *are* the human race. Our mother and father *were* the human race; and so are Uncle Eeak and Aunt Zoo-Zoo. You aren't going dotty, are you my dear? You frighten me by saying things like that!'

Yok Pok turned his head away from his sister's frantic scrutiny and said with a rather forced chuckle: 'Well, you see, my dear, that anything as important as one solitary man making up his mind to become the destroyer of all mankind is likely to be upsetting when you hear of it for the first time and from the actual person who is thinking it. But if you give yourself up to listening carefully while the person in question, that is to say I myself here, sitting opposite to you and talking to you, offers you all the various reasons to think over by which he arrived at his conclusion, his decision, terrific and crazy as it sounds in your ears when first announced, may take on quite a different aspect.'

Yok Pok's voice was so calm, and his expression so unruffled and undisturbed that Quo Pok could only bring herself to murmur, 'Well, the best thing we can do, my dear, it seems to me, is to sleep on it and over it, and when we've both considered the sort of shock you've given me, and when I've considered the various reasons for what you call your *decision*, which no doubt you will give me tomorrow, we shall both be in a better mood for understanding each other. Let us sleep over it, dear Yok, I beg you. Don't let's refer to it any more tonight.'

Yok Pok agreed to obey his sister and went to bed. But it was some time before he could go to sleep. 'Why,' he kept asking himself, 'have I decided to put to death the whole human race?' His answer was definite. 'Because my conscience tells me it's the right thing to do. My conscience tells me that if I don't destroy the human race the present slaughter of animals for food and the torture of animals by these appalling vivisectors will increase and increase. When once there isn't a single human being left alive on this earth the animals will be free. They may kill each other for food, but they will all have their young to look after; and the cows will give their calves their milk and the birds will build nests for their little ones and feed them with what they like best to eat, and all the fish, whether in salt water or fresh water, will be in no danger from the hooks of those abominable anglers and will be able to escape or unable to escape, as destiny or chance may decree, from the sea monsters who swim about seeking their natural food. Have I,' Yok Pok asked himself, 'enough of that smoke-bomb I discovered three years ago in the cellar of Castle Rumpus? It could have finished off the whole damned lot of us. It certainly did for those three old beggars who used to bother me so much on the woodpath to Castle Rumpus. I never knew where they were from, and when I asked them the only person who told me anything was a gypsy girl who said they came from Austria. But that smoke-bomb certainly finished them off. One moment they were standing begging and the next they were lost in a cloud of smoke that seemed to carry them up into the air. I only used a handful of the bomb-dust on them; and now I've got hidden, in a harness loft that Quo doesn't know about, enough to do for every man, woman and child in this whole bloody world, if I could get an aeroplane far-sighted enough to carry me, and it with me, over the whole surface of our globe.'

Yok Pok couldn't help thinking to himself before he went to sleep as if he were talking to someone else. He was always like that. It was what made him so trying a companion. But their parents had died so long ago that his sister had had to get used to it. Yes, she had had to get used to his tiresome trick of announcing every detail of his private thoughts as if it were a speech from the throne to which all listeners had to give respectful assent. Yok Pok evidently felt that before he would be able to slide peacefully into a beatific ocean of

2

Yok Pok slept a deep and long sleep; but so far from this absolute escape from consciousness having the effect of relaxing his resolution and diminishing his decision, when he awoke about eight and rose from his bed simultaneously with the rising of the sun he was, if possible, even more determined to extinguish the race of mortals to which he belonged than he had been when he went to sleep. 'Yes, I shall do it,' he told himself. 'There's enough bomb-sand or bomb-dust or bomb-secretion in my harness-room — and I'm not yet sure I took all there was in Rumpus cellar — to blow to smithereens the whole bloody spawn of Adam and Eve. I could cry like a babe,' he went on, and tears as big as the eggs of hedge-sparrows did drop from his eyes upon the floor as he bent to pull out the chamber-pot from under the bed, 'when I think of the animal revolution I am going to bring to pass. Yes, there shan't be the smallest dwarf with two arms, two legs and a squeaking phiz left alive on the earth when I've finished my job. Every animal, every bird, every fish, every reptile, every worm, every insect, shall lift up to heaven such a scream of ecstasy that the other planets will think disease and death have been abolished for ever upon earth. I know very well what Quo will say,' his thoughts ran on. 'She will say, "What about yourself? Don't you belong to the human race yourself?" And what shall I answer to that?'

He sat down on the edge of his bed and rested his sharp

chin on his clenched knuckles and his sharp elbows on his knees. What crossed his mind was a triumphal ceremony in which all the friends and relations he possessed were gathered together for slaughter and after having killed them all he would kill his sister Quo and himself. 'The great difficulty,' he said to himself, still seated on his bed in intense thought, 'will be the steering of the aeroplane on which I shall fly all over the earth.'

It was then that he suddenly thought of his Great-uncle Eeak, an extremely eccentric old gentleman who was very rich and who always told them that his wife, their Great-aunt Zoo-Zoo, had Jewish blood and was descended, centuries upon centuries upon centuries removed, from a cousin of the grandparents of Jesus Christ. He also told them that there had always been rumours in Aunt Zoo-Zoo's family that they were descended from a person not so dear to Christians as Jesus, but perhaps even more dear to polytheistical scholars with an obsession for all early legends about the human race, from nobody less in fact than Penthesilea, Queen of the Amazons. 'I wonder,' he said to himself while his forehead pressed violently upon his knuckles and his elbows so violently upon his knees that he almost groaned with pain, 'whether Uncle Eeak would lend me his aeroplane and explain to the men who run it that they must obey me. Would Great-uncle Eeak be so angry at the whole idea that he would call upon his wife Zoo-Zoo to curse him with the curse of her centuries-removed cousin Jesus of Nazareth for his presumption and wickedness in regarding the descendants of Adam and Eve as less precious than the creatures with which Noah filled his Ark? Wasn't this the very curse with which Jesus lambasted the Scribes and Pharisees, not only for their hypocrisy but for behaving so differently from the Good Samaritan towards the weak and helpless and for bringing their wretched business cheats into the holy temple?'

Yok Pok had never dressed more rapidly than he did that morning and had never hurried off more hastily to the house of his Great-uncle Eeak. Eeak was not a rabbi though his head was full of rabbinical learning, and the constant presence of Zoo-Zoo and her intense interest in all that was religious and ritualistic gave him a daily and nightly delight in discoursing on these things. Yok Pok was shown into his Great-uncle's study by his butler, Ur Veer, who might well have acquired the dignified art of his important office in a training at the palace of a Pharaoh.

'Zoo-Zoo is out shopping,' were Uncle Eeak's first words after Ur Veer had closed the door, 'but she will be back soon. She's always pleased when you visit us.' Eeak's study seemed made of dark mahogany and heavily laid-on gilding. Pictures, chairs, tables and even the edges of an enormous bookcase were all richly and heavily gilded.

There were three armchairs, one facing a richly burning coal fire and one on each side of it. The two latter were evidently intended for Eeak and Zoo-Zoo, while the guest faced their hearth; and it was facing this beautiful red fire that Yok Pok now stretched out his feet, his toes erect, his heels firm against the fender.

'I think you agree with me, Uncle Eeak,' he said, 'more than anybody round here, about the wickedness of this awful vivisection of animals that these confounded scientists love to excuse on the grounds that it benefits humanity. I think it does just the opposite. Yes! I think what it really does is to encourage our bloody doctors to experiment upon their patients when they get ill, just as these accursed scientists do on these unfortunate animals. I tell you, Uncle, half the things they do to us these days are purely scientific experimentation. They want to know more about the insides of men for purely scientific reasons, not in order to save their human patients from pain and suffering.'

'Yes, my dear boy, I do agree with what you are saying,' replied Uncle Eeak from the depths of his comfortable armchair. 'I would sooner be shot dead by a murderous burglar than have scientific treatment from a scientific doctor. You see, my child, this age of ours is the most degenerate age we have ever endured since the days when David killed Goliath and Samson brought that temple down, or was it a theatre, on the heads of all those enemies of Israel. O what happy Christmasses we used to have when my grandfather was the Vicar and I was a youth with a host of brothers and sisters! In those old days clergymen were like consecrated policemen who went about their parish with a pocket full of shillings; and policemen were like competent schoolmasters who went about threatening poachers and burglars and highwaymen with having to "bend over" and be birched or caned into proper behaviour. Clergymen and policemen were the rulers of country places in those days, while the roguish old Squire in his big house thought only of how many foxes he could hunt and how many pheasants he could shoot. Nowadays the government thinks it has done nobly for a village when the Squire has to earn his income tax by showing tourists over his big house while he and his family live in the lodge and send their gamekeepers to Australia and their sons to Canada and their daughters to New York to find American husbands.'

Yok looked at his rich relative with respectful silence for a moment. Then he went on: 'I know *you* agree with me in my feelings about all this sad change, Uncle, but most of the people I talk to think things have greatly improved; and that in the old days the majority of folk were simply the working-class who had to earn their living while the upper class enjoyed itself by killing foxes and deer and birds and fish. I know you do agree with me, Uncle, in all this. But what I want to ask you now is a special and particular question. You own an aeroplane, as they call them, don't you Uncle Eeak?'

Eeak smilingly acknowledged this weakness. 'Yes,' he replied, 'and I often fly in it. Its name is Irah. It has, or she has, two men, extra skilled in our grand new art of flying, who in themselves are captain and crew. They are bosom cronies and have been so from their childhood, though they are cousins, not brothers. Their names are Kar and Lar.'

For some reason, that although he tried to analyse it, Yok Pok couldn't get to the bottom of, there was something about the names of these two cousins, Mr Kar and Mr Lar, who were so good at flying the Irah whose name Uncle Eeak pronounced Ire-Rah, giving it the emphasis that would make it the ire or wrath of some mysterious great person called Rah, yes, something about the names Kar and Lar that caused him profound discomfort. Was it perhaps that, although Uncle Eeak might possibly accept without question the murderous use to which he had decided to apply the Irah, Mr Kar and Mr Lar were likely to indignantly refuse to consider such a proceeding for a single moment? 'Shall I,' he asked himself, 'explain fully and completely to Uncle Eeak what I have decided to do; and then leave it to him to deal with Kar and Lar?'

3

Yok Pok finally came to the conclusion — and it took him more than a couple of days and nights to arrive at it — that it would be wiser to keep it dark from his uncle until that gentleman had placed him in command of the Irah and allowed him to set off with Kar and Lar as his subordinate officers.

In spite of having reached this conclusion Yok Pok still felt a certain uneasiness, which a little disconcerted him until he had the spirit to tell himself that what troubled him was the attitude of Aunt Zoo-Zoo. Ever since he first spoke of the Irah to his uncle, he had begun to notice that Aunt Zoo-Zoo frequently regarded him with a queer expression of unsympathetic if not actually hostile mistrust.

She was a formidable lady; much more formidable as a woman than his Uncle Eeak was formidable as a man. Had his Uncle told her all that he had been talking to him about? Had she detected with the perception with which Nature, the Mother of us all, has endowed women, especially old maids, that there was more in his trip — if his Uncle allowed him such a trip — than he had confessed to Uncle Eeak? Thus a most agitating question arose in his mind. Should he — could he — dare he, actually reveal what was in his mind to Aunt Zoo-Zoo? No! It would be sheer madness to do such a thing — but *would* it be? Or was he on a completely wrong track in this line of thought?

The discussion about the aeroplane Irah between Yok

Pok and his Uncle Eeak still went on while Yok Pok remained there on board arguing as cleverly and as subtly as
he could with Kar and Lar and not allowing the vessel to
leave port or set out for any purpose or destination till he
had done his best to reason these two young men into his
way of thought. His sister Quo was a great help to him in
this difficult enterprise as she was such a young and pretty
girl, so slim, and so exquisite in her ways, that it soon
became clear that neither of the young men was anxious to
leave their harbour if it meant leaving little Quo behind.

But meanwhile Auntie Zoo-Zoo became more and more
dissatisfied with everything. She was about forty and her
love for her husband Eeak had been the chief thing in her life
since she was four and he was five. She had never had a love
affair and she had never wished to have one. She idealized
her husband and imagined that he was a far greater man than
he was. She was thrilled when he purchased Irah and she
made up her mind that she would use it at once to pursue the
chief purpose of her life, which was to put an end forever to
the infernally cruel practice of vivisection. Her influence,
for she was an extremely persuasive and magnetic person,
and her presence, for she was a remarkably handsome
woman, had always had a great effect on Yok Pok and Quo
Pok. They had no difficulty in blindly accepting her idealization of Eeak but their respect for herself was a thing they
had taken for granted from their childhood and they never
especially emphasized it or enquired into it.

Zoo-Zoo herself, however, forty as she was, had never
allowed her youthful enthusiasm for the double legend of
her ancestry to die out. She was still constantly thinking of
the tale that she actually had in her veins the blood of the
family of the Madonna, the Mother of Jesus, and — to
herself anyway almost equally thrilling — that she was
descended from Penthesilea, the Queen of the Amazons.
Zoo-Zoo had always possessed — from her earliest girl-
hood and in spite of her frantic idealization of her husband
Eeak it persisted still — a profound belief in the superiority

of women over men. She had steadily refused, and did so now that she was forty as passionately as she had done when she was fourteen, to cease meditating upon the life of the Queen of the Amazons. She had no idea whether it was usual for school-teachers to reveal to young girls in their early age the basic secrets of sex. But, usual or not, there was a teacher at the village school to which her parents sent her who took a delight in emphasizing these secrets. She didn't do it in public in the class. She did it in private in her own bedroom which was in the school, for she came from Paris and none of the other school-teachers had any idea whether she was a lonely orphan or whether she had a host of relations there. Her name was Ripple-Pipple, and nobody but herself and the pupil she was teaching in her bedroom knew what she taught or how she taught it. It must have been the effect of her lessons that the girl she instructed revealed nothing of it to her parents but did discuss these lessons with passionately shameless interest with other girls of the same age who had been similarly instructed. The Head Mistress of the school where Ripple-Pipple taught was Miss Goldenguts, and Miss Goldenguts, without talking about it, always felt a little uneasy when she saw Miss Pipple's pupils whispering furtively to each other. 'Can she,' Miss Goldenguts would ask herself, 'can she possibly be a Lesbian?' Miss Goldenguts was herself so far from being a Lesbian that the greatest moments of pleasure in her life were when her cousin Lar brought his cousin Kar to have supper with her. This the two lads did even after they had begun living on their aeroplane lying at rest at present on the landing at the port; for Miss Goldenguts was an extremely good cook and knew to a nicety the sort of dishes that boys like best.

Quo Pok had been to Miss Goldenguts' school and had been instructed by Miss Ripple-Pipple, and if anyone had dared to ask her where she learnt what Miss Goldenguts always called 'the Facts of Life' she would always speak of Miss Ripple-Pipple as 'one of the teachers' and never mention her name. Quo Pok had as a matter of fact been emboldened so much by the intimacies of her sex lessons as to dare to ask Miss Pipple how it was that she was baptized Ripple. And Miss Pipple told her frankly, 'Oh that is because I had a cousin called Ripple who came from Upwey, a village near Weymouth in England where there's a sacred fount where a Saint — I forget his name now — made the water run when the whole countryside was perishing of thirst. It's a place not far from an estuary where swans had their nests and where my Uncle once gave me a swan's egg which I took back to France and kept in our cellar till the rats devoured it.'

Auntie Zoo-Zoo had a very strong prejudice against Miss Goldenguts' school and she never approved of her niece Quo Pok being educated there. She would never display any real politeness towards Miss Ripple-Pipple, in spite of the fact that she knew well that she came from Paris. What caused her a curious and queer feeling of real jealousy was what she heard from the gossip of neighbours about Ripple-Pipple of Paris and her sex-lessons; but some secret resentment in her nature forbade her to ask her niece Quo Pok any questions about Mademoiselle Ripple-Pipple.

One evening after she had been talking to her husband, Uncle Eeak, for a long time about their nephew Yok and their niece Quo, Aunt Zoo-Zoo sat down in the little room upstairs which she called her Boudoir and gave herself up to a fit of quite elaborate introspection. 'What is it in me,' she asked herself, 'that makes me so shrink from the idea of having a baby? I know well that Eeak never dared to "take" me, as we say; but that was a peculiar fear he had of "taking" a girl, though he loved me from the bottom of his heart. He had no idea, and still has no idea, of the curious horror I had of childbirth. We were a queer pair in those things; a very queer pair, when you remember that we were really in love with each other. But the truth was' — and so searching and daring were Auntie Zoo-Zoo's thoughts that she got up from her armchair and went to a mirror hanging on the wall and tapped with her knuckles the reflection of her forehead, and then, returning to the armchair, she stretched out her legs and clapped her hands to her face — 'the truth was that though we were in love we were both obsessed by the same nervous mania, an unnatural horror of natural fornication. What would I have done,' her thoughts wandered on, 'if I had been Penthesilea's youngest child? Would I have protested when my mother told me I must let myself be "had", as we say, by some handsome young Greek, knowing perfectly well that when he had "had" me, or when he had lived with me long enough for me to give birth to a baby girl, she, my Mother, would have him put to death?' Aunt Zoo-Zoo's mind then veered to her Bethlehem legend. 'Were all the relations of Joseph and Mary as nice as Mary's mother, Saint Anne?' Aunt Zoo-Zoo pulled in her long legs and crossed her hands above her knees. 'The legend in our family always said, my mother used to tell me, that it was from a cousin of Saint Anne's called Rebecca that we are descended. Eeak was saying only last night that the best of having Jewish blood is that there is no other race in the world that holds the family, to which any man or woman or boy or girl belongs, as the most important thing about them. Jewish carefulness about money is, Eeak reminded me, an essential part of their family feeling.'

Auntie Zoo-Zoo pondered in her mind every aspect of her present situation and grew, the more she thought of it all, less and less pleased. 'Yok Pok and Quo Pok are sweet kids,' she told herself, 'but I'm not content to devote my life to nice youths and maidens solely because I happen to be their aunt. What *have* I got at the back of my mind that keeps pricking me on larger, grander, far more exciting and far more daring undertakings than just petting a couple of youngsters and helping them to enlarge their minds?

'Eeak doesn't really understand me at all,' her thoughts ran on. 'Of course he never really did. No, not even when we first fell in love with each other. I knew he didn't, but that didn't bother me; and as to having children, we were just the same. We both had the same neurotic and morbid dread of the sexual act. I just worshipped Eeak, and I do still reverence and respect him, but I would not have him know what my thoughts are about myself for anything. He would be shocked and horrified and deeply disturbed. He would probably be seriously hurt in his feelings. For I am sure he just thinks that I admire the spirit with which he just takes for granted that because I was so desperately in love with him when we started living together I must be quietly and happily and peacefully congratulating myself that he has never turned away from me or wanted to live with any other woman. How quaint and curious it is that it never occurs to him that I should want to be great and famous myself quite apart from him. I suppose that is the difference between men and women. Men must all want to be great and famous and must feel that compared with women they are intended to be so, and that nature intends women to take this for granted and simply to feel happy and proud that nature has allowed them to have found for their mate in life a man whose greatness will go down to posterity. It is interesting to think,' thus did Auntie Zoo-Zoo's meditations run on, 'how few women there are in the history of the human race who have become world figures of renown compared with men. It is no use for us to say to ourselves that the two great rulers of human life, Destiny and Chance, have always found it easier to bestow their gifts upon men than upon women. Nature evidently takes for granted that the place for women is in the kitchen while the place for men is wherever their instinctive ambition and power working together have the strength to project them.

'Now what,' thought Auntie Zoo-Zoo, 'could I do to make myself and my name famous forever?' She stretched herself out further and clasped her hands tighter. 'Suppose,' she said to herself, 'that I had the power of becoming in my own person the great goddess of the Earth about whom I learnt so much at school. Gaia was her name. I remember that very well indeed. She was so persecuted by the embrace

design of theirs. 'I wonder,' Auntie Zoo-Zoo said to herself, 'if I have got in me the power of enlarging not only the magic and influence of my presence, but my actual physical size? Oh I would so like to turn myself into a giantess of such terrific size that I should tower over everybody and when people saw me approaching they would cry, "Oh take care, take care! Here comes that terrific goddess! Take care lest she eats you up!" '

As she said this to herself she suddenly became convinced that she did possess this power; and she deliberately began to use it. It only felt to her as if she were pulling her muscles together as she used to do some thirty years ago when, as a child of ten, she began a tennis match. Yes, she found she could do it. She felt as if she had a godlike force within her that could enlarge her body just as if with pencil and paper she could make a female figure she was drawing larger and larger and larger. Her body soon began to get so large that her feet reached to the wall and the armchair on which she was sitting became like a little object sticking fast to her bottom. She rose to her feet and found that the top of her head bumped against the ceiling. Her breasts had become so big that her blouse hurt them and with her two strong arms and hands she tore the thing from her and flung it in tatters upon the bed. Then Auntie Zoo-Zoo decided that the moment had come for informing her husband Eeak what had happened to her; but she decided it would give him too great a shock if she appeared before him without any warning and she told herself that the wisest thing to do was to summon Quo Pok and make her her messenger. It was now just nine o'clock p.m. Where was Quo Pok? Had she gone to bed? Auntie Zoo-Zoo decided to call her. 'But I mustn't shout. My voice would be too loud,' she told herself. 'Perhaps if I just whispered a simple whisper from this colossal chest of mine might sound as loud as a shout.'

Auntie Zoo-Zoo had judged correctly. A whisper from her did turn out to be as loud as a shout; and soon she heard the airy-fairy steps of Quo-Pok tripping down the stairs.

Then the colossal lady, as she now was, acted very wisely. She opened the door but held it firmly by the handle, keeping it only a little ajar. When Quo Pok knocked she spoke to her through this inch wide entrance, whispering as softly as she could. 'You'll get a shock when you see me, my dear. I've been praying hard to heaven to turn me into a giantess: and heaven has done so and my size will startle and shock you. But though my appearance and even my voice may startle you I am just the same old Auntie Zoo-Zoo I always was. What I wanted you for was to ask you to go to Uncle Eeak's study and tell him what I have done to myself, or permitted heaven to do to me. Tell him he must be prepared for a shock; but tell him I am just the same Zoo-Zoo underneath it all. Will you do this for me, my darling? You might come down with him too for I'd feel easier about it if I had you both in the room with me. I'll sit on the floor and hug my knees when you enter. I expect I'll look less frightening if I do that.' Quo Pok gave a rather forced little laugh, for she was evidently nervous; but she replied at once, 'All right, Auntie, I'll come down with him.'

Uncle Eeak and Quo Pok entered together and found Auntie Zoo-Zoo, as she had announced she would be, seated on the floor, hugging her legs. 'Oh my dear,' cried Uncle Eeak, 'how could you do this, or make heaven do it?'

'I'm sorry, my dear,' said Auntie Zoo-Zoo from her seat on the floor, 'but it suddenly came into my mind that the best way of dealing with these cruel scientists who practise vivisection purely for their own experimental interests and then pretend when we attack that they do it for our good, would be to give them a shock. And it came into my mind — I thought it was sent there by Providence — that if little Quo Pok's Auntie Zoo-Zoo turned into the great heathen goddess Gaia the Earth, who was forced by the embraces of Uranus the Heavens to give birth to a series of appalling monsters, it came, I say, into my mind that if I could get Providence to make me big enough to resemble a great planetary goddess, when this set of cruel vivisectors were preparing to set out on this diabolical quest of theirs to collect animals to vivisect from the shore of the planet Venus, whose torture would be a great triumph for these fiendish men, it would be a shock from which some of them might never recover if I could appear before them as a giantess of terrific size and declare myself to be the Goddess Gaia now returned to her place in the world after an absence of a couple of thousand years, and I should feel that the shock I gave them would be empowered by the ghosts of all the animals they had vivisected since this accursed practice began. Of course, Eeak darling, you must ask Kar and Lar if they don't feel it would be possible for me to ride in your Irah at a little distance from the coast until these cruel vivisectors set out in their aeroplane and then rush upon them; so that they would see me in my present gigantic shape rise up from Irah's deck, and not only see me but hear me shout their damnation in such a thundering voice as will make every family living along the coast think that the Day of Judgment has arrived.'

Uncle Eeak was undoubtedly deeply impressed by the words of his transformed spouse; but it was clear to little Quo Pok that he was still suffering from such a terrible nervous shock by her changed appearance that his usually calm and collected mind found it no easy task to function in its accustomed manner.

'You're not afraid, I hope,' the lady went on, 'that my weight will be too heavy for the Irah? That indeed would be a stumbling block to my plan. Perhaps in that case I might manage to swim, for as you know, Eeak dear, I can swim, holding on to the Irah, and then, when we were close to them, I might rise out of the water and scare them so much by my appearance that it would be easy for Yok Pok who, I learn, is ready for battle, to dispose of them in his own dire way.'

'Little did I dream,' thought Eeak, 'when I married Zoo-Zoo, that a girl who claimed to admire me so much and who was as much in love with me as I was with her would ever do a thing like this to herself or make Heaven do it. But, since it's done, it's done; and I certainly shall be glad I bought Irah if through her, and between us all, we do manage to send these appalling vivisectors to play their little games at the bottom of the sea.'

It was at this moment that Yok Pok himself came on the scene, followed by Kar and Lar. He had been to his store in the harness-room where he had put his precious explosive discovered in Rumpus Castle; and he now carried it in an enormous coal-sack over his shoulder. He was startled but not frightened by the sight of Auntie Zoo-Zoo turned into a colossal giantess; and he promptly began discussing with her and Uncle Eeak how they could most speedily destroy this crew of notorious vivisectors on their way to the planet Venus to collect their animals to torture. 'My practical difficulty,' Yok Po explained to them all as they sat round their enormous Auntie Zoo-Zoo in Uncle Eeak's dining-room, 'is how to snatch my handfuls of explosive from my sack if I keep it hanging round my neck as it is now.'

'Why not cut a hole in the centre of your bag?' said Kar, so that you can stick your hand in and pull out a handful of the stuff whenever you want to?'

'But more will come out, like that,' said Lar, 'than you want, and you won't be able to stop it coming out.'

'What makes your stuff explode?' enquired Auntie Zoo-Zoo from the position on the floor which she still preferred to make her throne.

'Oh just its contact with the air,' replied Yok Pok. 'I found that out when I stole it from Rumpus Castle. I killed three fellows with it who used to annoy me by begging from me at a particular place in the wood. It's just the rush of air when you throw it that makes it explode. And then it just blows what you're aiming at up into space. There is no fire or smoke, only a sort of cloud.'

'What I would suggest,' said Auntie Zoo-Zoo from her position on the floor, 'is that you let me sew on to the side of the bag a big loose sleeve into which you could thrust your arm and pull out a handful of the stuff whenever you need it. I could sew one sleeve on to the side of the sack so that you could thrust your arm down it and pull out one handful of the stuff after another; but I could sew it, I think, in such a way that the stuff would not come trickling out when it was not required.'

'Have you got a needle and thread up here in this room, Zoo-Zoo?' enquired Uncle Eeak.

'Certainly I have,' his wife replied, 'if you'll hand me my work-basket. It's behind that inkstand and it's got that sleeve of my old dressing-gown folded on top of it.'

'Shall I put my sack down there by your side on the floor,' enquired Yok Pok.

'Yes,' she said, 'by all means do so; only we must be a bit careful in case a gust of wind comes down the chimney, as we've got no fire in our grate today.'

Very carefully this huge giantess into whom Auntie Zoo-Zoo had been transformed sewed a loosely hanging sleeve to the rough sack at her side, a sleeve made of a material sufficiently heavy to hang down from the sack in such a manner as to keep the sack's contents from slipping out into it. 'When you've got your sack round your neck, Yok,' she told him, 'don't forget to arrange it in such a way as to make it easy for you to slip your arm up the sleeve I have sewed on without having to twist your neck too much!'

'I sure will,' replied her nephew, 'and oh I do thank you so very much, Auntie, for taking all this trouble. Please Heaven we'll be able to give these devilish vivisectors a good sound lesson tonight or tomorrow.'

'I think we shall,' murmured Auntie Zoo-Zoo hugging her knees after helping him arrange the sack. 'But I think I'd better stay on the land and not weigh down your Irah with my weight.'

As he pondered on board the Irah about all these things it was not long before Yok realized that their discovery about this particular plan of these unspeakable vivisectors had rather modified his original decision to make this voyage a pitiless crusade against the whole human race. 'Something like that,' he said to himself, 'may come of it; but the first thing for us to use the Irah for is to destroy every single one of these infernal vivisectors.'

Yok Pok experienced a certain element of relief in feeling that now, with this immediate narrowing down of his problem to the destruction of a set of cruel devils whom all his friends and relations hated just as he did, he was making war against the wickedness of his race rather than against his race itself. He took up his abode on the Irah and though he had several rather violent arguments with Lar and Kar, he also had several very friendly talks in which they all offered new and original suggestions as to how to go to work when their enemy's aeroplane appeared on the scene. Nor was it very long before this actually happened. It was from a port known to the world in general as one of the most historic in British history that the vessel hired by the vivisectionists, a vessel whose name was *Adamant*, came up the coast, collecting special little groups of 'Sworn Tormentors' from many townships as they publicized their quest. These grand looking gentlemen, for in their minds they must have possessed the same sort of conviction of personal righteousness that Calvin must have had when he burnt Servetus, and that Torquemada must have had when he ruled over the Spanish Inquisition, allowed themselves to anticipate with luxurious and unctuous satisfaction the newly designed tortures they were preparing when they returned with their captives from the misty shore of the planet Venus.

The clash between the infernal vivisection vessel Adamant and the thrice blessed animal rescuing Irah occurred at about eight o'clock in the morning of the twenty-second of January 1960. Auntie Zoo-Zoo, now transformed into Gaia the Goddess of the Earth, had begged her husband Uncle Eeak and the two lads, Kar and Lar, to allow her to stretch out at full length on the upper deck of the Irah; and all three had given their proud consent. It goes without saying that Yok Pok derived indescribable pleasure from the ease with which he was now able, thanks to Auntie Zoo-Zoo's so carefully adjusted sleeve, to draw all the explosive dust he required out of his sack at any given moment. The moment came when the vivisectionists from the prow of the Adamant called out their challenge to all on that shore. Yok Pok's arm shot down the carefully prepared sleeve into his sack and brought out a big handful of this terrible essence of all the explosive powder in the world. Then when the prow of the Adamant approached the edge of the landing-stage where the Irah lay, with Auntie Zoo-Zoo stretched out on her back along the deck, he flung the powder at the approaching enemy. It exploded in the faces of a group of the vivisection leaders who were calling their challenge to the line of the coast as they floated in. Every one of this group was blown into the air and they were carried upward in such a cloud of mist and smoke that it looked to Uncle Eeak, as he watched from his bedroom, as if a swarm of sojourners from Hell were desperately invading Heaven. The Adamant was ordered by its other commanders not to risk any further attack from this dangerous coast, for they evidently didn't realize that it came from an aeroplane in the water near the landing-stage, and without further delay they flew off towards the evening star which was still just visible, though only just, in the light of dawn.

'After them! After them!' cried Yok Pok.

'You'd better come with us,' he added to his sister, for it was clear that delicate little Quo Pok was hesitating whether to mount into the air with them or to stay at home.

'Please come, Missy!' cried Kar and Lar with one pleading voice. And that cry from the two lads did decide her. She nodded and smiled and went to stand near her brother, while Lar and Kar went down into the engine-room to make their aeroplane follow the Adamant into the brightening evening sky.

Uncle Eeak smiled sadly as he watched from his bedroom window the Irah follow the Adamant into the air. 'I might have had the child to myself,' he thought, as he watched the two aeroplanes ascend, carrying his wife with them.

The Irah was soon only a mile or two behind the Adamant as they ascended together in the direction they wished, though the sun was now brightening the whole sky and Venus with the other stars and planets had totally disappeared.

Auntie Zoo-Zoo pulled herself together and sat up with her heels beneath her and her knees bent, leaning her back against the midship rail. The day slowly passed. She had her meals; she had her evacuations. She had her strolls from end to end of the vessel. Then the night descended; the stars came out and the planet Venus once more showed herself. As they mounted higher and higher, following the lights of the Adamant, which were visible above them and remained at about the same distance away, Auntie Zoo-Zoo had a very weird and frightening experience. She was crouching by the rail of the vessel when she became aware of three snouts emerging from the water and breathing against her face.

5

The awful thing about these three snouts or appalling faces was that they all three murmured the word 'Mother'. Then in a flash Auntie Zoo-Zoo realized what it meant. By persuading Heaven to make her so big, and by thinking of herself as the goddess Gaia the Earth, she resurrected and brought back the horrors as well as the glories of that lost, ancient and forgotten world. And now it all came back to her and she knew who these three awful beings were. 'Gorgons and Hydras and Chimaeras dire' — yes, it came back to her how Ouranos and Uranus had begotten these monstrous beings upon her; until in her desperation she had given her son Saturn a sharp stone of flint in order that he might cut out the genitals of Ouranos or Uranus. This he did; with the result that out of foam thus generated in the sea Venus Aphrodite was born and brought to shore at Cyprus.

So it now happened that as she leaned against the rail of the Irah, with gusts of cloud-foam sprinkling her at intervals, she was forced into contact with each of the three monsters whose father was Ouranos or Uranus. 'If I gave birth to you,' she said to the Gorgon, 'why is your face so hideous? My face is the face of an ordinary woman of the Earth, all the strength and richness, all the depth and delicacy of the Earth I can feel within me, why then, oh child of my womb, is your face so indescribably hideous?'

'Your thoughts must have been like my face as you let my father have you!' answered the Gorgon.

'Why did you let Hercules slaughter me?' asked the Hydra of her. 'I was your child, wasn't I? You can't deny that, can you? What a cowardly mother you were, then, to let all my beautiful serpents' heads, seven of them, remember, seven of them! be torn off by that great, muscular, rampaging brute?'

And then came a third voice, the voice of Chimaera: 'And you only pretended to be my mother, you swollen-bellied bitch! My mother was Echidna and it was that bully, that wandering, blustering rogue Bellerophon who killed me! Neither you nor your confounded Uranus had anything to do with me! You want to be the mother of all the world, don't you, you big harlot?'

'Well,' thought Auntie Zoo-Zoo to herself, 'I certainly undertook a laborious job when I projected myself into the personality of Gaia the Earth-goddess. But I never thought I pretended to be the mother of other people's monsters!' She summoned Yok Pok to come to her. 'Can't you make your lads Lar and Kar run this aeroplane a bit faster? I don't see why we shouldn't overtake that confounded Adamant. Wouldn't it be better if you could kill off with your explosive every living man on the deck of that blasted plane?'

'They'll lessen their speed, Auntie, don't you worry, when they get near Venus. The mist round her is so thick that our poor old Irah won't have to go any faster to catch them up; and once we're on a level with them I'll finish them off, all of them, the whole damned lot, don't you make any mistake! But we must get level with them, don't you see, before anything like that can be done.'

'Well,' replied Zoo-Zoo, 'it's all a wild game, and whether we kill them in time to save those Venus animals is still a bit of a gamble. But I think we shall win. I think the odds are in our favour. When we've finished them off then we can say with Catullus — it is Catullus, isn't it? — "Soles occidere et redire possunt. Nobis, cum semel occidit brevis lux nox est perpetua et una dormienda." '

The Gorgon, the Hydra and the Chimaera, all three,

returned to the air, through which apparently they intended to follow the Irah till she overtook the Adamant. Little Quo Pok whose slender figure struck her Auntie as touchingly slight and slim when she stood by that new Gaia's side, asked what would happen if her brother Yok did succeed in killing all the vivisectionists on board the Adamant. 'Shall we all have to land on Venus, Auntie?' she asked: 'And if so, what shall we do with the plane of those cruel vivisectionists? Shall we have to leave it stranded on Venus or will Kar and Lar be able to tow it all the way back to the Earth behind us? And if they do that, will you and Uncle Eeak be able to keep both planes?'

'You must remember, my dear,' replied Auntie Zoo-Zoo, 'that these wicked and diabolical vivisectionists have headquarters all over Britain. They don't only live in our coast towns. They torture animals in all our big cities. Their grand excuse is that they do it for the advance of science and for the benefit of patients in hospitals who will gain by their discoveries. Pain and nervous terror and the exquisite quivering of exposed nerves and all the horrible experiments which delight these infernal sadists are done, they will calmly assure you, for the benefit of science and of medicine and for the curing of patients in hospitals and the supplying of both night and day nurses and all hospital authorities with valuable information. Until our government passes an Act of Parliament making all vivisection illegal and ordering the police to enter these premises and arrest the men who are practising it, this monstrous thing will continue unsuppressed. What we deserve will very likely soon happen to us. The masters of scientific vivisection will dominate the human race. They will do to us what hitherto we have allowed them to do to animals. In fact, in certain directions they have already begun to do it. Very soon the rulers of this world will be a group of so-called scientists who will establish — finding no difficulty in finding architects to build it — a universal scientific inquisition, the rulers of which were pre-figured and pre-

dicted by Edgar Allan Poe when he wrote: "Mimes in the
form of God on high mutter and mumble low and hither
and thither fly — blind puppets they that come and go at
bidding of vast formless things that move the scenery to and
fro and flap from out their condor wings invisible woe." '

Auntie Zoo-Zoo had only just finished quoting Edgar
Allan Poe's verses when her delicate little niece Quo Pok,
leaning at her side against the same rail, suddenly
whispered: 'Did you hear that, Auntie? Something's been
happening down below. I heard Kar and Lar and I heard a
strange man's voice.'

'You go and see, my precious, you go and see! And come
back and tell me!'

The slim little girl scrambled to her feet, hurried to the
ladder and disappeared. Auntie Zoo-Zoo listened intently,
putting everything else out of her mind. Yes, she did hear a
stranger's voice, a man's voice, and a deep-throated formidable one! 'I'd better stay where I am,' she said to herself.
'Little Quo will soon be back.'

And so she was. 'Oh Auntie Zoo-Zoo!' the girl cried. 'He
was hidden down there when we started. He's a big man.
Yok told me to tell you he'd bring him up to talk to you in a
minute. He's a big man!'

And in a moment there he was, led to her side by Yok Pok
and followed by little Quo and soon after by Kar and Lar.
The stranger was indeed 'a big man'. He was about six feet
in height, and he had a very large and commanding head
covered with curly brown hair. His nose was aquiline, his
eyes deep-set, a dark greenish blue in colour, and separated
from each other more widely than is usual. This was emphasized by the fact that he had no eyebrows at all. His ears
were minute in proportion to the size of his head but they
were very delicately formed, and every now and then, if
you watched his face carefully, they seemed to quiver, as if
listening to sounds that nobody else could hear. Auntie
Zoo-Zoo looked up at him from her seat on the deck and
boldly asked him his name. 'My name is Ki,' the man

replied. 'I pronounce it to rhyme with cry or shy or fly, not with flea or bee or tea.'

He knelt down very politely at Auntie Zoo-Zoo's side and laid his hands upon hers, which were folded round her knees. They looked closely for a moment into each other's eyes. 'Why did you come?' enquired Auntie Zoo-Zoo.

'That's just what he won't tell us,' said Yok.

'Yes, we can't get it out of him,' cried Lar. 'Though we've tried every way, haven't we, Quo Pok?' echoed Kar.

They all crowded closely round the two figures, one seated and one on his knees. At last Auntie Zoo-Zoo enquired whether they had got a berth for Mr Ki below stairs. Yok Pok replied at once that they had. 'It is a berth, but it is more than a berth; it's a small bedroom. It's where the captain of the plane used to sleep; the fellow from whom Uncle Eeak bought our Irah.'

Auntie Zoo-Zoo restrained a natural desire within herself to ask more questions about this 'captain' or boss of the Irah before her husband bought it. She knew that for long there had been a great many things that she had never asked Eeak about, just as there had for long been a great many things that she had taken good care he shouldn't ask her about. 'It must be so,' she said to herself now, as she stroked one of Mr Ki's knuckles with the little finger of her left hand, 'with all elderly or middle-aged married people when the passionate desire of early love to tell all and hear all has been outgrown. I must,' she continued to herself, 'have some talk with him up here before he goes to bed and before I go down to our boys' lounge to get more sleep than I can get up here.' Then she spoke aloud to Yok Pok. 'Take the boys downstairs, will you, Yok, and show Quo where you've got that little cupboard for her to sleep in you told me about when we first came on board. Leave me here to chat for a few minutes with Mr Ki and when I do come down to sleep in the lounge, beg the boys to leave for me to wrap myself in that big thick blanket I brought with me from home.'

Yok Pok promised to do just what she wanted; and he

went down with his sister and the two boys and left her alone with Mr Ki. 'We were destined from the start of things to meet like this,' said Ki to Auntie Zoo-Zoo.

'You have expected it for many years?' enquired Auntie Zoo-Zoo.

'Since I was ten,' replied Ki. 'A voice in my innermost being said to me once when I was playing with a large teddy bear in Ay House, Dorchester, Dorset, "You shall rule the world if you do what I tell you." I called out in answer, holding the teddy bear high above my head; "I will, I will, I will, I will!" Then the voice said: "You must say to the moon and the sun and all the stars: Obey me! Or in every vein there shall be pain and in every head a weight like lead." "Whose voice are you?" I asked, for you see I was only ten when it spoke. "Yours! Yours! Yours! Yours!" said the voice. And being only ten I tried it on my brothers. And they each cried out: "It hurts! It hurts! It hurts! It hurts! It hurts!" Then I said to the voice, "Do you mean that the veins in the sun and moon will hurt and the head of the sun and the head of the moon will feel as heavy as lead?" "No," said the voice. "What I mean is that all the creatures who live on the sun and the moon will feel a terrible hurting and their heads will feel like lead." "If they don't do what I tell them?" I said. "Yes," the voice within me answered. "If they don't obey you that is what they will feel." "But what shall I tell them to do?" I asked the voice within me. And the voice replied, "Recognize me as your lord and king, forever and ever." You see, my dear lady,' Mr Ki went on, 'what I have not yet confessed to you is what the voice finally said to me. "You are to be the ruler of the entire universe," the voice said. "You are to be King of the World. But in order to be this utterly and completely it will be necessary for you to have a Queen. This Queen need not be your wife. She need not even be your mistress. All she must be is your Queen, the Queen of the Universe, just as you are its King." The voice went on more definitely still. It described you to me. It told me where I could find you. You must understand, dear lady, that the older I grew the more I obeyed the voice within me. It told me that you were already married and that your husband would own this aeroplane from which you and I as King and Queen would rule the entire Universe and go travelling around it, commanding the allegiance and obedience of every galaxy of stars we visited.'

Mr Ki gazed passionately into the eyes of Auntie Zoo-Zoo and she returned his gaze. Up and up towards Venus they went and Ki's words turned out to be true; for so dense was the mist — what in Welsh is called niwl — all around Venus that the Adamant was forced so to slacken her pace that Irah was soon at her side. Then Yok Pok had his chance. Into the sleeve of his sack went his arm. Blow up! Blow up! Blow up! And every vivisector on board the Adamant was whirled into the air in a cloud, yes! a whirly-whistly-windy-waggly-wiggly cloud of human fragments.

It was not long after this that Ki, with a golden crown on his head and Auntie Zoo-Zoo with a golden crown on her head, set out on their world-tour of visiting all the ports of call in their obedient Universe. Ki was so clever at arming himself that what with his steel and gold and silver and copper and leaden accoutrements he brought it about that he and Zoo-Zoo, enormous as she had become, didn't differ an inch in height or in breadth from each other. They rode on Irah; and behind them came trailing Adamant, closely towed in the rear under the direction of Yok Pok and Kar and Lar, who had no difficulty in managing both planes thus connected together.

6

King Ki and Queen Zoo-Zoo came to love each other so
well as they toured the Universe over which they ruled that
they finally had a child. This child was called Why. They
had a long and sometimes almost angry discussion as to
what name to give their infant. They agreed that the name
must begin with the letter W; but Ki liked the name What
and Zoo-Zoo liked the name When. At the moment their
difference was at its height Zoo-Zoo suggested the name
Where. This rather pleased Ki and in the subsequent recon-
ciliation it was after Zoo-Zoo had, without thinking of any
name, simultaneously asked the question 'why' about
something King Ki had said that they agreed that they
would call their child by that name. Why was a boy, and it
was when he became nine years old that the great event of
his life occurred. He suddenly decided that he was weary of
this life of following his royal parents to every portion of the
Universe over which they ruled, and he boldly turned to
them when they were all three together and asked whether
they would allow him to go off on an exploring expedition
of his own. King Ki and Queen Zoo-Zoo looked at each
other with considerable dismay. She thought: 'I would like
to have a private conversation with Ki before letting the boy
go,' and he thought, 'I expect the best thing to do would be
to tell him to fly back to the Earth and explain to him how to
dodge the sun and the moon on his way there.' But Why
was too quick for them both. 'Don't fly after me, Dad,' he

said, 'for that will only make me fly the faster and I know I can outstrip you. I will come back, Mother dear, for sure, so don't worry or let Dad worry.' And with that he was gone, circling round the nearest galaxy as swiftly as a swallow and soon completely disappearing from their sight.

'He'll come back all right, my dear,' said Ki quietly. 'He's a wise kid.'

'Heaven grant he will,' gasped Queen Zoo-Zoo. 'I don't think we ought to have let him go.'

Why was soon far past the nearest galaxy and away off into the growing darkness. 'I must find,' he thought to himself, 'some completely new world, something I can really tell them an exciting tale about, and I have an instinct that I will.'

The last thing that Why expected to happen, as is the case so often in life, was the thing that did happen. It had already become so dark that the only stars he could see were a few faraway, tiny sparklers, when suddenly he saw somebody or something flying straight towards him.

'By God!' he murmured. 'It's a boy!' He was quite right. It *was* a boy. Each of them had been rushing through space as if they had been swimming at a terrific speed through a dark ocean. Now they stopped and faced each other, flapping their hands and stamping their feet so as to retain the same position.

'Me be speech reader,' said the strange boy to Why. 'Me read other-world thoughts. Thy mind be English mind so speech-reading me say English words to thee.'

'Where do you come from?' enquired Why.

'From I'm, yes, from I'm,' replied the other boy. 'I come from the great, wonderful, noble, mighty, unequalled, immeasurable, indestructible land of eyes and mouths which is called I'm.'

'What do you mean by a land of eyes and mouths?'

'Feel me on both my front and my back,' said the strange boy. Neither of them had any clothes on, so this was easy. All down his front from his chin to his toes were very small deep-set eyes shielded by enormous eyelids which to Why as he passed his hand down them, felt like the wings of large butterflies. 'And feel my back, young Master English,' said the stranger. Why obeyed; and it was a real shock to him. All the way down the boy's back there were open mouths, each with lips and teeth and a tongue. Why was glad enough not to have to feel any more; but he couldn't resist saying: 'Where is your prick and your balls?'

'On my side, at my hip,' replied the other. 'Yours, I suppose, are in the front?'

'Yes,' responded Why gently, praying in his mind that the other boy would want to feel the aforesaid sexual organs. 'I suppose,' Why said, 'a girl's quim would be just opposite the prick and balls at your side?' The other boy chuckled naughtily. 'I certainly hope so.' Then Why said, 'I don't believe my parents, King Ki and Queen Zoo-Zoo, have ever seen your country of I'm, and if you don't think me rude to ask, will you please tell me your name?'

'My name is Ve Zed,' said the boy. 'My father's name is No Zed and my mother's name is Yes Zed and I have a grandfather still alive whose name is Well Zed. My father has always been careful not to annoy him in any way; but my mother feels differently about that.'

'I suppose in my English way of talking your land of "I'm" is pronounced so that it rhymes with time?'

'Yes,' replied the Ve Zed, 'you've got it quite right. The "I" part refers to the eyes in my front and the "M" part refers to the mouths in my back.'

'But wouldn't it have been much easier,' said Why, 'to rape your wife when you marry, or your girl if you get a mistress, if the sexual organs of both of you had been in the front part of your bodies?'

'I know what you mean,' replied Ve Zed. 'You mean it must be rather a queer job to squeeze and push my begetting-spear up her quim and through her maidenhead by just cuddling and pressing her sideways? I expect you feel it would be impossible to "take", or to "have" a girl, as we say, unless you did it front to front?'

'Yes, Yes! That's just exactly what I *do* feel,' cried Why. 'Of course what the big boys of our land do at school, if they prefer being naughty with a boy rather than a girl, is to push their prick up the boy's bottom. That's what nowadays people call being a "homo", rather a silly name, as *homo* is the Latin for a man and the old Romans were much more addicted to loving women than other men. But the ancient Greeks were different. Socrates was condemned to death by his government for corrupting the lads with whom he fell in love.'

'Would you like me,' said Ve Zed in an almost caressing and coaxing voice, as Why's allusion to Socrates had made him feel as if he lived under Pericles and Aspasia, 'to take you to my home in I'm? I am sure both my parents would love to meet you, and I wouldn't be surprised if my grandfather Well Zed didn't come round to see you if he heard you were there.'

Why agreed at once. He had already been feeling, before he met Ve Zed, a little lonely and desolate; and the idea of being installed for a few days or even a few weeks in this country of I'm of which his relatives had never heard satisfied his spirit greatly.

It took the two boys much longer than Why had expected to reach their goal. 'No wonder,' he thought in his heart, 'Father and Mother have never seen this place. I would never have seen it if it hadn't been for meeting Ve Zed.' And then, as they flew side by side, using their arms and legs as if they were swimming, Why suddenly asked Ve Zed what had set him off on this long flight from I'm towards the planet Earth. 'I'd got tired,' was the answer, 'of hearing Father and Mother argue about old Well Zed and of Mother always telling Father that her family was much older and more mythological than his. I thought that if they let me fly to a different part of space altogether I would see and hear things that would enlarge my viewpoint and teach me more about life in general.'

'And they did let you,' said Why.

'Yes, they did, but it took some while to persuade them. It was Mother's always bringing back the topic of the greatness of her ancestors compared with the Zeds that prolonged the delay of their permission.'

'Who were her ancestors?' enquired Why, thinking in his heart, 'I mustn't bring up the cousin of Our Lady or Penthesilea, Queen of the Amazons.'

'They were,' Ve Zed replied, 'a sister of St Helena, the Mother of Constantine the Great, and a man whom that sister married. The man's name was Bobby-Up and he was a descendant of the famous Daedalus, the father of Icarus, but from an early love affair of this great artist-inventor before Icarus was born. Bobby-Up was a creative artist of extraordinary power, and it was his power and genius that my mother used to tease my father about, insisting that it was superior to anything possessed by any of the Zeds. My mother always declared,' went on Ve Zed, evidently with a desire to beguile their visitors from the earth into taking his mother's side in this ancestral dispute, 'that Bobby-Up invented a chemical substance which had the power of attracting to itself the remains of ancient worlds, long-forgotten galaxies of stars, which in the remote distances of space still hung about like scattered dust floating this way and that way in the vast emptiness of the immeasurable void. The effect of Bobby-Up's invention was that this substance, by drawing to itself by degrees the floating atoms of vanished worlds, was able to thicken out in space a resurrected mass of pregnant matter that gradually became the body of a new world, a solid productive body, full of the diffused juices and essences of grains and fruits and plants and roots and seedlings and sucklings and the scattered rudiments of upward-springing vegetation. Thus did my mother's ancestor, Bobby-Up,' Ve Zed went on, 'create the vast body of a new world, a body that filled a reeking gap in the Universe out of which not only vegetation could spring but so far unknown beasts and birds and reptiles and so far unknown creatures resembling men and women.'

Why and Ve Zed flew on together happily now that they had come to know each other, and it was a really exciting moment for Why when he was led into his new friend's house.

There was only one kind of tree in I'm and the name of that tree was Urb. It was short in height but of colossal girth. In fact it was twelve feet round and its branches weren't branches in the sense of branching out. They were short, upright sprigs, about half a dozen of them together, each with one round cup-shaped leaf on the top of its upright spike, a leaf that when it rained, as it did regularly once a week in the middle of the afternoon at I'm, became filled to the brim with dripping water. No Zed, Ve Zed's dad, was tall enough to stand up to one of these Urb trees which grew just in front of their door and drink from their cups, each of which contained about as much water as a teacup.

But it was the inside of Ve Zed's home that captivated Why most. The house contained only one level ground-floor room. But this room was very large and the interesting thing about it was that in place of chairs, though there were bookcases, and on the floor a series of richly-coloured ex-tremely thick rugs, there were beds, some designed for two people, as could be seen by two pillows side by side, and some for only one person. Why was offered a seat on one of these beds, and on the bed next to him Ve Zed flung himself down on his back. They all spoke English and Why decided that the first thing he would ask them, when the stir of his arrival had subsided a little, was how this had come about.

Mr No Zed and Mrs Yes Zed were both soon talking to Why. Mrs Zed was sitting at the foot of her son's bed, tenderly loosening the tennis shoes he had been flying in and stroking his feet; while Mr Zed was sitting by Why's side and had begun to show him an enormous folio, half of which rested on the visitor's knee and the other half on his own. The book was illustrated by pictures of palatial interiors that reminded Why of pictures he'd seen in various churches and cathedrals and also in museums in London. But it was only the statuesque and prehistoric look of this book that made him think of the Louvre in Paris, the National Gallery in London and the Prado in Madrid. When, however, Mr No Zed turned its pages all was otherwise. These fronts of ferocious mouths and these backs of waving eyelids, and above all these improper, ill-adjusted fantastical side-way bursts of hipping fornication, soon made Why realize that the land of I'm was no resuscitated archaic Agora of Pericles.

'Where did you all learn to speak such good English?' he flung out at them. Mr No Zed and Mrs Yes Zed exchanged a word or two together that sounded as if they felt that 'The Jabberwock with eyes of flame, came wiffling through the tulgey wood, And burbled as it came.' But they were now interrupted and Mr No Zed had to snatch the folio up, close it with a bang, and lay it on an empty bed.

Into the room rushed Grandfather Well Zed, bringing alarming news. 'There's an attack on us! The King of Kanawitakon has sent his son Gee Wizz, the Admiral of the Kanawitakon Fleet to attack us! No attack could be worse! These men under Gee Wizz are like madmen. They run and jump and gyrate the windmills without anything but their sails! There's no standing up against them. Their cruelty is the talk of our country. In that war between Kanawitakon and Kokaloo, as soon as Kanawitakon won, what did it do? Your generation is too young to know. But though I was only a lad then I can tell you. They took all the members of Kokaloo royal family and buried them in the ground up to their necks, leaving only their bare heads exposed in a long row. Then the same Gee Wizz, only he was much younger then, danced forwards and backwards from head to head along that line of heads! Those buried men with their heads exposed and their eyes looking about them remained like that till they all died. They talked to each other and they didn't die all at once. Get ready all of you! Get your swords

and staves and shields and spears! We've got to fight Gee
Wizz and these mad Kanawitakans until we've driven them
out!'

It was then that Mrs Yes Zed went up to the old man Well
Zed and whispered to him of the presence of Why, the son
of King Ki and Queen Zoo-Zoo. The old gentleman didn't
hesitate a moment. He walked straight up to Why and
begged him to face these invaders and order them out.
'Your parents, my boy, would support my word,' he said.
'We have all recognized them here in I'm as the Rulers of the
Universe.'

Never to the end of his life did Why forget the scene that
followed. He signed to Ve Zed to accompany him, which
the young flier bravely did, and the two lads rushed out of
the hall together. I'm was a land of promontories and
estuaries and the hall out of which the boys rushed was on
the bank of a harbour up which the barges of the invading
Kanawitakans were now forcing their way. At the prow on
the front of these barges stood Gee Wizz. He was a man of
about thirty. He was grotesque in his appearance; for he was
very tall and thin but he had an enormous head and face, and
at the ends of his long thin arms and legs he had colossal
hands and feet. He was now brandishing a huge battleaxe
and as Why and Ve Zed rushed to meet him it occurred to
Why that it must have been with a weapon like this that
Bellerophon set out to slay the Chimaera. Gee Wizz swung
it round his head and then swaying his whole thin body to
make the blow effective he smote at the two boys as they
advanced side by side. It was clear that Gee Wizz with all his
warlike experience knew nothing of the instinctively quick
movements of young boys; for both Why and Ve Zed
slipped down on their knees like a couple of pygmies
attached to Achilles; and the great axe sweeping over their
heads crashed into the base of the impenetrable rock upon
which the Zed citadel had been erected. The whole rock
with the majestic building upon it quivered and shook from
top to bottom. Still waving in triumph the handle of this

axe, though the blade of it remained embedded deep in the great rock which it had nearly cleft in two, Gee Wizz, followed by all the wild crews of all the barges of their now grounded fleet, rushed up the slope to the great Hall at the brazen gates of which the whole historic squadron of Zedite guardsmen waited to hew them to pieces. Before the battle began, however, there suddenly appeared from the south the aeroplane called the Adamant. It was flown by Yok Pok and his sister Quo Pok alone. As can easily be imagined, Why, the son of King Ki and Queen Zoo-Zoo was full of joy to see such a propitious arrival at this moment of moments, for it looked as if the Zed-guardsmen at the gate were not strong enough to resist the attack headed by the terrifying Gee Wizz.

He expected to see exactly what he did see. Yok Pok signed to Quo Pok to go down below and touch some knob or some handle; and the girl, stepping easily and lightly as she always did, obeyed him to the letter. Then he thrust his hand down the long sleeve so carefully and so skilfully fastened to the mysterious sack which he kept slung over his left shoulder. Down went his arm; and up came his hand full of the explosive powder. Into the air he flung it, and in the explosion that followed something like half a dozen of those murderous invaders vanished in a whirling, upward-flying cloud of grey mist. Again Yok Pok's arm sank into that sleeve and again, as the powder flew from his hand a second time, half a dozen sturdy naval veterans were lost in that ascending vapour of death.

It was when it had become quite clear with the arrival of the Adamant, with Yok Pok and Quo Pok on board and the former armed with that terrible sack of destructive powder, that the attack on the Zed citadel was doomed to fail, that Why Ki and Ve Zed instinctively drew together.

'I am getting sick of all this killing business,' said Why Ki.

'Come then, my friend,' said Ve Zed boldly, 'Let's go off by ourselves! We got on before quite beautifully flying together. And now if we just become obedient slaves to the folk here, or obedient slaves of your Daddy Ki and your Mummy Zoo-Zoo, we shan't have anything like the feeling we had then.'

'Besides,' agreed Why Ki, 'what none of our relations realize is that fellows like us, after having once tasted independence aren't made by Nature to sink back into the old domestic round of doing what our "elders and betters", as they say, tell us to do.'

'Come on then,' cried Ve Zed. 'Let's fly straight off now, over there! Yes, above all this damned flat land in front of us, and leave it behind, and fly, side by side, as we did before, into unknown space.'

The happiness which these two youths, Why Ki and Ve Zed, derived from their flight together, when the land they left behind vanished from their sight and all that remained of the galaxy to which Venus and the earth and the sun and the moon belonged were faint streaks of red light and little sparkles of white light, was a happiness such as neither of them since they were children had ever dreamed of enjoying.

7

Happy as Why Ki and Ve Zed were, as they flew along side by side into infinite space, they were neither of them oblivious of the terrific enormity of their adventure. Nor did any sign appear as they flew side by side, using their arms and legs rather in the manner in which swimmers use them but much more easily, carelessly and casually.

'What will happen to us,' said Ve Zed to Why Ki, 'if we go on like this, with no sign of any stars anywhere and without meeting anything?'

'Well, I suppose,' answered Why Ki, 'we shall get so tired and so hungry that we shall decide to stop flying altogether and let ourselves sink, making no motion at all, sink down and down and down, like a couple of dead bodies. We could hold hands, so we wouldn't be separated; but otherwise just sink, sink, sink, sink, and let fate decide upon what planet or into what world we shall come galumphing down.'

'Well, my dear,' said Ve Zed to Why Ki, 'from what I feel, and I expect you feel much the same, there's something in me that seems to say, fly on, fly on, fly on, fly on, and let happen what will happen! I don't feel really hungry myself, and I bet you don't either. Nor do I feel really tired, and I'm sure — yes! I can feel it through your hand — that you don't either. So let's go on, old friend, till we both are certain sure that our flight must be brought to a finish.'

Why Ki responded to this by tightening his grip on the other's hand, and on and on and on and on they flew. Then there suddenly was a change, a change of the most astonishing kind, a change in themselves.

'Are you there?' said Why Ki to Ve Zed. 'Why have you dropped my hand?'

'You dropped mine!' replied Ve Zed. 'But I don't believe we've got any hands any more! What the devil, my dear, has happened to us?'

'It seems to me,' said Why Ki, 'that we both have become bodiless! It must be a crazy dream, a mad dream, a nightmare, due to our long flight through all this empty space.'

They were both silent; but they flew on, each still trying to hold the other's hand. Then, still completely bewildered by what had happened, the whole change came over them; and not only so, but they knew they were now in the midst of a large crowd of people in exactly the same situation that they were in themselves, only more used to it. One of these people, a young girl of about their own age who evidently realized that they were newcomers and consequently caught in a cloud of dazed bewilderment, came gently and tenderly up to them.

'Don't worry about your bodies, laddies,' she said to them; and it was her presence, combined with the obvious fact that she had no body, that baptized them into a realization of the situation. 'None of us,' she went on, 'nobody here has any bodily form. What has happened is that we are all now pure minds, thinking, imagining, analysing, speculating, pretending, dissenting, agreeing, disagreeing, discerning, philosophizing, recapitulating ideas, expressing ideas, developing ideas, denying ideas, revealing original intuitions and clarifying individual self-deceptions. You must realize, dear boys, that what we all are here and now is a galaxy not of stars or planets or suns or moons or meteorites or comets, but simply and solely of floating intelligences, yes, of bodiless minds crowding about one another and struggling each of us to express our individual thoughts and ideas. What you must understand, my dear lads, is that none of us here have any senses — we

Let me tell you two boys about my last conversation with my uncle. "Well, my child," he said to me, "there'll be nothing more for you now than this crazy country we're in now, this country in infinite space which they tell me is called Tappaskulltinkadom." At that I cried out to him, "Take me with you, Uncle! I'd sooner be dead with you than alive in a country like this. To be dead is to be dead. It's the end. No intelligent person believes any more in all this silly talk about God and the Devil and heaven and hell. You were alive and now you are dead, and that's the end of it. You've been very good to me, Uncle, and I honestly thank you for it. I've learnt a lot from this voyage with you into space; and it certainly has been amusing, lighting upon a fantastical country like this absurd Tappaskulltinkadom. But I'd sooner be dead and done for with you, Uncle, than live to be a hundred in Tappaskulltinkadom, with my ideas growing bigger and wiser and subtler and truer for years and years and years! You have carried me into space, Uncle, and are now dying in space. Oh Uncle, let me die with you! I've been alive. Life is an experience. But I've had enough of experience. The beauty of death is that it isn't experience. It's just simply nothing. You were, you are not. You never will be again. And you don't want to be again. Life is interesting, Uncle, I don't deny it. And death is wholly and entirely devoid of interest. I don't deny it. But when we've had the interest of life, that's enough. Now let us have the opposite of interest. Let's have the divine and delicious dullness of death." But as you boys can well imagine,' Nelly Wallet went on, 'when Uncle did die and I had done exactly what he had told me to do, that is to say bury his body in this confounded Tappaskulltinkadom and ordered the men on board his plane to take it back where it came from with the quickest speed possible, I did all I could to compel this blasted place to mean something to me. I made no attempt to make friends. For everybody seemed to be far too occupied with spouting forth their ideas and floating up and down in trances of mental contemplation, or in ecstatic enjoyment of their own cleverness, to want to bother about somebody else's ideas or somebody else's thoughts, or even with somebody else being there at all. In fact I very soon became convinced that if you could be what is called *selfish* about enjoying your senses and eating and drinking and tasting and smelling and hearing and feeling and seeing things you liked, you could be still more *selfish* about displaying and trying out and indulging and enlarging your ideas and thoughts. Another thought has come to me of late,' Nelly Wallet went on, 'and that is how delighted many moralists would be at the complete absence in this skull-thumping, idea-worshipping world of sexual pleasure. Apparently it never occurred to the creatures of Tappaskulltinkadom that few things lent themselves more enticingly and ecstatically to long brooding thoughts than the delicate art of masturbation. Why, among all these thinkers, among all these brooding ponderers upon the thoughts that can fill a self as a self meditates upon itself, has no missionary of exquisite provocation advocated a prolonging of the adorable spasms of masturbating abandonment? Why has no habitual practiser of the more than voluptuous extension of the paradisiac organ of the imagination when the self alone with the self prolongs the self-play of luxurious erotic saturation, ever advocated his practice here?'

Our two lads, Why and Ki, looked at each other with extremely puzzled expressions. They had always taken it for granted that masturbation was as much a prerogative of young men as menstruation was a prerogative of young women. And anyhow, what in the name of all the worlds in space, was the part to be played in this mad game of life by somebody dwelling in Tappaskulltinkadom, where all the senses had to be relinquished and only thought was allowed, who wanted to enjoy, even if unshared by anyone, nothing but long-drawn-out indulgences in the most absorbing sense of all, possessed by all living creatures, the sense of sex?

Then suddenly an inspiration came to Why Ki and he boldly said to Nelly Wallet: 'What is there about this life in Tappaskulltinkadom to prevent my becoming an ardent advocate of sexual thought? It is surely an idea of some length and breadth and height and depth? As an idea to be advocated by me as if I were a missionary of Buddhism, or of Mohammedanism, or of Christianity, it is surely in accordance with the fundamental principles of Tappaskulltinkadom that I should from now on set about advocating mental and spiritual masturbation?'

Nelly Wallet replied at once. 'What you are confusing in the back of your brain, my dear Why Ki, are two quite different and separate things: the first is the idea which we were all as children, wherever we come from, instructed by our elders to accept, namely that sexual thoughts are wicked and ought to be blotted out from the mind that dwells on them. The second is that the suppression of sexual feelings is the sign of a puritanical mind, a mind whose ferocious and savage hatred of sexual pleasure has caused one of the largest and most genial fountains of human sympathy that we possess to dry up at the source.'

'What would you yourself, my dear Nelly,' murmured Ve Zed gently, 'best like to do if you became our permanent companion?'

She answered without a second's hesitation. 'I *am* your permanent companion,' she said. 'I decided to be so in the middle of last night, and what I want to do with you is to leave Tappaskulltinkadom forever and to fly on and on and on until we reach some world as different from this as this is different from the Earth from which you came.'

As can easily be believed the result of this conversation was that during no more than the next five minutes they were all three flying together hard and fast in the most extremely opposite direction from the one that would have led them back from Tappaskulltinkadom to the Earth. On and on and on and on and on the three of them flew together. The girl flew between the two boys who now and

again would touch each other's hands across her back, as if
to indicate to each other that their acceptance of her as their
sister was absolutely mutual. On and on and on and on and
on and on they flew. Then what they all three were sure
would eventually happen did happen. They were in another
world. They knew it from the presence of two phenomena.
The first of these was now suddenly beneath them. Yes,
there it was! In place of the darkness of aerial space
stretching indefinitely and infinitely away from them in
every direction, there was now Something beneath them.
What was it? Oh it would have been so hard to describe it to
anyone who had not been with them and felt its presence! It
resembled, they told each other later, a circular landscape
like an enormous globe composed of half-frozen water
which was sufficiently solid to make them aware that its
presence beneath them had taken the place of the emptiness
they had grown used to. This globular orb was made of air
and water and ice, and it gave them the clear, un-
questionable feeling that they were floating above a
rounded world whose surface sloped up and sloped down,
just as if it had been a colossal soccer ball projected by some
lively immortals at each end who were using space as their
playing-field.

'But who lives here?' enquired Ve Zed of his two friends.

'I think there's one of its inhabitants squatting on my left
instep,' replied Nelly. 'Could either of you catch it with
your fingers?'

'I'll have a try,' said Why Ki. 'There, I think I've got it!
But it's a very little thing!'

Little no doubt it was, but both the boys were soon able
to examine it and to hold it near enough to the face of their
adopted sister for her also to examine. This was rendered
possible by the object itself, who carried with it, or wore
upon it, a shining blaze of light by which they could all three
look at it and look at one another as they did so and at the
surface of the world they had reached. It was then that the
little creature spoke to them.

their hands and their toes pressed against the surface of Orb, and Nelly kneeling upon Orb while she pushed back her hair from her forehead, one of these little balls, out-breathing and in-breathing with more energy than the others, came and sat on the back of Nelly's hand as she tidied her hair.

'You three must realize,' it said, 'that your appearance is a very important event in the history of Orb. We have no language of our own now. But quite apart from our readings in ancient Greek and Latin and our pleasure in modern English, we sometimes wonder whether it isn't possible that there is far away from this present universe of infinite space dotted by thousands of worlds completely unknown to one another, a universe as different from this one as our Orb and we who inhabit it are different from the other worlds and their inhabitants which you have visited in your journey. Don't you think it is possible that long ago, perhaps what you would describe as a million years ago, there came down here from another universe a group of space-travellers who expressed themselves as we do today by breathing in and breathing out, but in such a way as to form the actual words of a memorable language, a noble language, a musical language, a subtle language, a language with infinite complexities and intricacies such as was able to express the thoughts and feelings and ideas of Beings far more divine than any race we know or you know today. Our universe with its infinite space, dotted with countless worlds such as you have seen and we have never seen and countless others such as neither of us have ever dreamed of seeing or ever will see, may it not possibly be a mere pygmy of a universe compared with the one that visited us a million years ago, or rather whose travellers visited us. Think of any human being's ways, feeling, prejudices, loves, hatreds, speculations, lasting a million years. And think of an Orb's units lasting the same length of time, so that you as you are and we are, can discuss life as we are now discussing it. Wouldn't it be marvellous if such were the exact truth?

And why shouldn't it be? I tell you, oh earthly travellers, the mystery of life goes deeper than your world or mine, deeper than our universe or any other universe, even than one a million years old.'

'Isn't it funny,' said Nelly to her two boy friends, 'that we should have arrived at this world of mind and ideas before reaching the end of space? You'd think it would be at the very end, and be the last word about human life.'

'I suppose,' cried Ve Zed, 'that we've made a great mistake in thinking for a moment that space can have an end. Space *must* be infinite, surely, my dears? It's the background, isn't it, to everything in the universe?'

'Is it necessary,' burst out Why Ki, 'that the universe should have a background apart from itself? Isn't space part of the universe? Isn't space as much part of the universe as a chair's legs are part of a chair, or an armchair's arms part of an armchair, or a floor and a ceiling part of the room to which they are the above and below?'

Nelly startled them both by what she said in reply to these two remarks. 'I've had a sudden vision,' she announced, in a low, calm, quiet and yet intensely earnest voice: 'Yes! I've just had such a clear, definite, decisive vision that it would be madness in me and wholly against my conscience not to describe to you.'

'Tell us! Oh tell us!' cried Why Ki. 'Tell us! Oh tell us!' echoed Ve Zed.

'Well, my friends,' said Nelly, 'I have just seen the *Wall of the World*. You can have no idea how clear, how natural, how vivid, how entirely real and how unquestionably there, this vision was! I could tell simply from its appearance that it was more than a hundred feet thick. It was built of rough, small, granite-like stones that had accumulated many tiny seaweeds between them which increased its look of solidity and antiquity and majestic impenetrability. It soared up till it was out of my sight and it sank down till it was out of my sight. It produced on my whole mind and body the effect of being the end of everything. I kept murmuring to myself, "The Wall of the World — the Wall of the World! This is the end of all." It was a faint grey in colour. And this greyness increased its impenetrable look of absolute finality.'

There was complete silence. Then very gravely Why Ki said, 'Let us leave Orb and all these round bits of Orb, each of which we could call an Orb-it as we escape its orbit, and let us fly on into space! Maybe, Nelly, we shall reach your Wall of the World as we fly on!'

'Goodbye, Orb!' cried Ve Zed.

Nelly agreed with a gentle murmur, and on they all three flew, the girl between them, with Why Ki on her right and Ve Zed on her left.

'When I said that the Wall of the World,' Nelly murmured as they flew, 'had little seaweeds between its stones, I think I was wrong. They were more like, as I remember them now, the small, grey patches of lichen which we've often seen on old walls at home.'

On, on, on they flew, and with nothing but darkness and space round them for so long they began to feel sad and tired. Then all at once there was a decided change. They were in twilight. This twilight swiftly brightened. They were in light, a light that came, as the two boys soon saw, from little crevices and cracks and holes in a great wall, the very wall which Nelly had seen in her vision. They all three stopped and clung to it with their fingers and their toes, Nelly still having Why Ki on her right and Ve Zed on her left. It was hard for Nelly to turn her head, as she would like to have done, first to Why Ki on her right and then to Ve Zed on her left. So all she could do was to talk to the former for a while, and then, after getting a firm hold on one stone with one hand and finding a deep slit for the support of one toe with one foot and pressing her forehead, though the little stones pulled her hair and hurt her, turning her head round to talk to the latter for a while. She was half-way between them, her face to the wall, and one of the little stones had caught her hair and was pulling it so that it hurt her, when they were all three startled by the sound of two ugly voices, extremely ugly voices, talking not so much *to* them, they all three felt, as *at* them.

'Hugger and Mugger are we, are we,
And we built this Wall for Posterity.
Architects both, and architects loth
To see their world dissolve like froth.
What will our Wall of the World keep out?
God and the Devil and rascals worse
Such as make all honest men rave and curse
To see what money they put in their purse!
Says Hugger to Mugger, "Our Wall goes down
Below the country, below the town."
Says Mugger to Hugger, "Our Wall goes up
Where Nebuchadnezzar can't get a sup.'

'I guess we three can disregard all this,' said Why Ki. 'And so, by Heaven, we will,' said Ve Zed.

'Let us sink down to the bottom of it,' said Nelly.

And both the boys clutched her hands, Why Ki her right hand and Ve Zed her left hand, and she led them in a reckless, desperate, abandoned drop, down, down, down, down, down, down, down, down, till they came to the bottom of the Wall of the World.

At that point they were confronted by an extremely natural problem: what to do next. The Wall of the World simply ended. It hung suspended in space. They had come down to see what had happened to it and what would happen to them. And now here they stood, all three of them, holding hands, Nelly between the two boys; and when Why Ki lifted up his left hand the tips of his fingers touched the bottom of the Wall of the World, and when Ve Zed lifted up his right hand the tips of his fingers touched the bottom of the Wall of the World.

Then suddenly both boys dropped their hands and both of them embraced Nelly and hugged her to their two hearts. 'If we were to plunge down into the darkness outside this wall,' said Why Ki, 'what would happen to us, I wonder?'

'We shouldn't be killed. We shouldn't die,' murmured Ve Zed. 'We should still be ourselves, wouldn't we? And we should still have Nelly.'

'Don't hug me too tight, my dears,' gasped Nelly, 'or I shan't have breath enough to tell you what I think. I think we are going to dive into Nothingness. I think that though we are here now, under the Wall of the World, and all three of us fully alive and fully ourselves, after we have agreed to do it, after we have made our plunge, we shall be a part of Nothingness, or, if you like to put it so, we shall *have been* three persons, two boys and one girl, who are no longer three in one, no longer boys or girls or any other sort of beings, but are as completely lost in Nothingness as if we had been black-beetles or bugs or fleas or frogs or toads or tadpoles or newts or minnows or sticklebacks.'

'Do you think, Nelly,' enquired Why Ki, 'that in every direction, all round all the worlds we have visited and all the worlds we have never visited, there extends this great mass of Nothingness? Does it extend to such a distance in all directions that it might well be said that, when the world is considered as a whole, far the larger part of it is Nothingness?'

It was then that Ve Zed burst out: 'But doesn't the Bible talk of God creating Darkness and Light? Then did God deliberately create a World whereof the larger part was Nothingness? Are we then to believe that it was God the Creator of the World who deliberately created Nothingness as the largest part of the World?'

'But, my dear Ve Zed,' protested Why Ki, 'Isn't God the Creator part of the World's Nothingness? Isn't the Bible only speaking of that little portion of the World that existed then and that still exists, quite independently of the much larger portion that has always been Nothingness? You must remember that if God himself was in reality only a part of the Nothingness of which we three are really a part, however we may think otherwise, then the creative God of the

Bible is now as much a part of Nothingness as we three shall be in a minute or two when we plunge into the abyss.'

But Ve Zed was by no means content with his friend's argument. 'But because we've reached the bottom of the Wall of the World,' he protested, 'is that any reason why you and I and our dear Nelly should die? Surely we could fly through empty space, avoiding every one of the worlds we've discovered, until we arrive at the world you came from, Gaia, the earth; and then you can show this earth and its chief city, which I was taught to call London, to me as well as to Nelly. You'd be thrilled, wouldn't you, Nelly dear, to tread the fields and shores of Gaia, and to walk through the famous streets of London about which they taught me such a lot at school, and you too I expect?'

'I don't like,' said Nelly nervously, and both the boys could feel from her hands that she was trembling, 'two voices I heard through the Wall of the World when I first saw it in a vision. The feeling I got from those voices was a feeling I've never had before and hope I shall never have again. It was terror, but it was much worse than that. It was disgust and loathing. But, my dears, please realize that it wasn't my vision of the Wall of the World that gave me these horrors. It was two voices that I heard behind it telling me they had built it. One called himself Hugger and the other called himself Mugger; and they kept on repeating an unending tedious dialogue, bawdily and grossly made up between them, and Hugger said one thing and Mugger said the other thing; and in all that they both said growing grosser and grosser and grosser and grosser and grosser, and more and more and more ridiculously stupid.'

'Well, Nelly darling,' said Why Ki. 'We three have to decide now, standing here together beneath the Wall of the World, whether we'd better plunge into the darkness beyond the Wall under which we stand and perish in nothingness, or whether we'd better remain safely this side and fly down together, avoiding every world that exists, until we reach Gaia, the earth; and find ourselves in the streets of London.'

9

But, as so often happens in life, whether in the life of human beings or in the life of the immortals, this terrific and terrible choice was not left to them. Striding towards them through the air came the greatest and strongest and tallest giant that any universe has ever known. It was none other than Gyges himself, a giant who possessed three arms. With one of these arms Gyges seized the base of the World Wall and shook it as if it had been the rail of a small staircase, until the whole thing began to crumble and fall to bits. Then with his right hand Gyges seized Why Ki and with his left hand seized Ve Zed, each by the hair of his head, and banged their skulls against the skull of Nelly until all three skulls became a congealed mass of blood and bones and brains which the Giant swallowed handful after handful until the three friends' heads were reeking in his belly, and the dust of the Wall of the World was scattered, along with their headless bodies, into every corner of space.

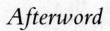

Afterword

The preceding stories were written towards the end of John Cowper Powys's long life (1872–1963). They are the last in a series of nine short fantasies that could well be described as the juvenilia of his old age. Nothing even in his own fiction quite prepares us for their bizarre character. But it does Powys an injustice to dismiss the stories as the playthings of a literary senescence: he welcomed second childhood, delighting in his rapport with the very young, and in these final tales he wrote simply to please himself, liberated from the world of 'adult' journalism, reviewers and literary critics (to which he had never in any case paid much attention). Unlike some other long-lived writers, John Cowper Powys seems to have enjoyed old age; it is one of the enviable, heartening things about him.

The son of a Church of England clergyman, and the eldest of a remarkably talented family of brothers and sisters — including T. F. Powys, author of *Mr Weston's Good Wine*, and Llewelyn, the philosopher and essayist — Powys developed relatively late as a novelist. He was an inspired lecturer and discovered ready audiences in America, where he lectured on English literature 1905–1934, usually spending the summers in England. He was in his mid-fifties by the time he wrote *Wolf Solent*, the book that established his reputation. Like the four novels that preceded it, this has a conventional plot with a twentieth-century background; but Powys was always as much aware of the timeless as of the contemporary, and his subsequent novels combine vivid evocations of particular places with a still more vivid sense of their psychic qualities — the products of history, of legend, and of the imaginative lives of their inhabitants. The last three elements became especially prominent in the two long historical novels, *Owen Glendower* (1940) and *Porius* (1951), written after Powys's retirement to Wales in his mid-sixties. These two books, together with the 'Wessex' quartet that had been published earlier — *Wolf Solent* (1929), *A Glastonbury Romance* (1932), *Weymouth Sands* (1934) and *Maiden Castle* (1936) — show him to be one of the major imaginative writers of his generation. The novels' range of characterization, incident, thought and emotion is complemented by an intricate pattern of imagery and a wealth of humour. Although not fantasies themselves, they deal with the genesis and power of fantasy; while in the Homeric world of *Atlantis* (1954) and the medieval one of *The Brazen Head* (1956), the miraculous and unexpected are predominant elements. For all their inventiveness and gusto, these two novels show signs of an imagination slowing down and circling garrulously round familiar preoccupations. In turning to space fantasy Powys cut his imaginative losses, and embarked on a genre that would allow his intellectual curiosity free rein.

Stylistically, the change in 'Up and Out' (1957), the first of these fantastic stories, is remarkable. Powys's opening sentences had tended to be circuitous and leisurely: now we have an aggressive, breathless start. 'Gor Goginog is my name and I am writing this in the English language for a special and peculiar reason.' Powys then launches on a succession of totally implausible events in outer space, in the course of which Moloch gnaws at the moon, eternity swallows time, God disputes with the Devil, and the narrator and his companions bring the book to an end by committing suicide. The most aggressive and bad-tempered of Powys's narratives, 'Up and Out' served him as a battering ram into a new fictional universe.

The other stories followed rapidly: 'The Mountains of the Moon' (published with 'Up and Out' in 1957), *All or Nothing* (1960), *You and Me*, *Real Wraiths* and *Two and Two*, the last three being written in 1959 and published post-humously. *You and Me* (which, like *All or Nothing*, is suffused by a nursery atmosphere) takes its characters to the far side of the moon and back; while *Real Wraiths* forgoes all pretence at human characterization in its account of the adventures of four ghosts in the company of, among others, the Devil, Hecate and Pluto. *Two and Two*, more intellec-tual in content, has as its central character an affable magician called Wat Kums, whose journeys in space on the back of the titan Typhoeus are quests for knowledge as much as adventure. Indeed, all these stories are so full of random philosophical speculation and wayward narratives that their inconsistencies have troubled some readers; their improvisatory qualities frustrate attempts at structural analysis. Powys's three final fantasies, published here for the first time, leave the reader no choice but to suspend logic and go with the free-wheeling fancy, or lose him altogether.

'Topsy-Turvy' was written towards the end of 1959, when Powys was eighty-seven years old. Its opening is reminiscent of a short story *The Owl, the Duck, and — Miss Rowe! Miss Rowe!*, published in 1930. This little fantasy had celebrated the life of various inhabitants of Powys's apart-ment at 4 Patchin Place in New York City, 'two of whom were human, two Divine, one an apparition, several in-animate, and two again only half-created.' In 'Topsy-Turvy' Powys brings to life his upstairs room at No. 1 Waterloo, Blaenau-Ffestiniog, where his own bookcase talks to his favourite books, and the rocking-chair of his companion, Phyllis Playter, goes 'ricketty-cricketty' down the staircase; it is a picture by his beloved sister Nelly, who died in childhood, which embodies the soul of Topsy. This eccentric story reflects the author's belief in the vitality of all material things; indeed, animism is a feature of many of the novels from *A Glastonbury Romance* onward. The eruption of Topsy and Turvy into the Other Dimension provides a clue as to how to understand the space travels portrayed in earlier stories. To Powys space is relative, not to be subjected merely to linear measurement. It is the intensity of Turvy's love for Topsy which brings them into the company of such diverse Powys heroes as Dido and Aeneas, Dick Turpin, King Alfred, Robin Hood and Edgar Allan Poe.

'Cataclysm' was written early in 1960. In a letter to Hal and Violet Trovillion, dated 16 February, Powys says that he is halfway through it, and that 'it is of absorbing and thrilling interest to me'.

> You see from my childhood when my favourite of all books was Grimm's Fairy Tales I have had an obsession or mania for inventing wild exciting impossible stories, the sort of stories that nowadays are called *Space-Travel-Fiction*.[1]

As in his Welsh fantasy *Morwyn* (1937), Powys's hatred of vivisection launched him on a visit to other worlds; but here no secluded Golden Age is discovered biding its time in the Underworld. Powys's imagination is ever straining up and out. 'Cataclysm' is the most vigorous of the final tales; and the enterprising Auntie Zoo-Zoo displays, in her wild way, Powys's sympathies with feminism. The story is a commentary of sorts on contemporary affairs, and it is therefore the more disquieting that it should end on a note of random horror, as though the author had suddenly wearied and despaired. Yet the message of the strange creature from Orb, that 'the mystery of life goes deeper than your world or mine, deeper than our universe or any other universe,' confirms the optimism of his earlier books, and belies this tale's conclusion. And in the person of Why Ki we have a recollection of the young John Cowper Powys as described in his *Autobiography* (1934), convinced that he was a magician.

[1] *The Powys Review*, Vol. IV, No. 2 (1984), p. 49.

'Abertackle' probably suffered as a result of Powys's attack of influenza in March 1960. The story falls into two virtually unconnected parts, exhibiting some forgetfulness and confusion. The first four chapters read like an elderly man's *Young Visiters*, the dialogue suggesting a kind of Mummerset devised by Harold Pinter; thereafter we are whirled off on another space adventure. This story is the most surrealist of the three, as when the Devil suddenly appears to be speaking from Powys's own room, or when the slaying of the mother–monster, Wow, slips from the narrator's account into a first–person recollection by the Devil. However inadvertently, Powys thus displays his awareness of the provisional and arbitrary nature of narratives: no wonder that earlier in the story he had referred to the master of fictional inconsequence, Laurence Sterne.

The stories are clearly improvisatory; the approach is that of the nursery tale, inviting an act of simultaneous creation on the reader's part, in which the question of belief or disbelief ceases to be relevant. The element of childishness, of 'suckfist gibberish' as Powys calls it, derives in part from Rabelais, of whom Powys wrote an illuminating study. If Dostoevsky is an earlier master, Rabelais takes over from Homer in the concluding period, in which alliterative repetition, rhetorical exaggeration and scatological humour are interspersed with intellectual and metaphysical debate. It is interesting to note that in these final tales the desire for, and belief in, a tolerant liberation of the senses still comes up against the taboos and repressions of late–Victorian England. The guilt over sexuality and aggressiveness which haunted the author's own life surfaces crudely and painfully: more than one pair of his characters fail to consummate their union. It is significant that Powys should use the violent words 'rape' and 'ravish' to describe the act of penetration. At least in 'Topsy-Turvy', the most genial of the stories, he allows the two dolls (in whose dialogues his own painful matrimonial situation is reflected) a fulfilment long denied to himself. In tackling this theme he reveals his

singular honesty: even in what G. Wilson Knight has described as 'sunset fantasies', Powys is determined to confront
this aspect of his experience.

Powys always insisted on the creative aspects of sexual
fantasy: what he writes in 'Abertackle' concerning the
magical fruitfulness of masturbation repeats affirmations in
All or Nothing, not to mention the more oblique in-
timations in *A Glastonbury Romance* and *Maiden Castle*. For
Powys sees all fantasy as potentially creative. In more than
one of these stories we find characters inventing a world.
Powys presents movement through space as a mental process; for space, like time, is relative to consciousness. In
Powys's world, space travel is a metaphor for imaginative
exploration.

The humour of these stories erupts in discordant absur-
dities, as when the Devil wishes he had grandchildren, or in
'Topsy-Turvy' Big Doll 'would even have said to the Holy
Ghost, if It had told him, "You are a Bloody Liar" '. Such
confident irreverence is perhaps a product of a clerical up-
bringing. The verbal high spirits evident in the use of puns,
alliteration, accumulative epithets and frivolous asides, like-
wise finds expression in the invention of farcical names: in
these three stories, following such earlier felicities as
Colonel Katterventicle, Thisbe Ranger and Lullaby Skim,
Powys offers us the raffish-sounding Jack Coffiny, Squire
Neverbang and a headmistress called Miss Goldenguts.
Here Powys's comic sense comes into full play in a manner
comparable with that of such (surprisingly close) con-
temporaries as Saki and Ronald Firbank. But the plainer
names of his principal characters recall the fictions of a very
different twentieth-century writer. Org and Asm, Why Ki
and Ve Zed, Gor and Wow suggest nothing so much as the
Clov and Hamm and Nagg and Pom and Pim of Samuel
Beckett.

And indeed, capricious though these tales of Powys are,
they yet relate to, and have a bearing on, the pessimistic
fables of the Irishman whose obsession with amputation

and confinement is as predominant in his work as the
craving for space and expansiveness in that of Powys.
Whereas in his trilogy Beckett becomes ever more intro-
verted in his attempt to prise their inventor from his fictional creations, Powys projects himself further and further
up and out and away from the self from which, as he
admitted in the *Autobiography*, he was perpetually in flight.
But he has none of Beckett's mordant bitterness about the
human condition: 'Born of a wet dream and dead by
morning' is not for him. Rather he would lose himself in
creation; to quote Beckett in *Molloy*:

> Not to want to say, not to know what you want to say,
> not to be able to say what you think you want to say, and
> never to stop saying, or hardly ever, that is the thing to
> keep in mind, even in the heat of composition.

Some such feeling may have determined the literary pro-
liferation of Powys's final years. None the less, unlike
though their methods and directions are, both writers are
concerned with the void that surrounds self-consciousness,
and with the impossibility of affirming that which is, except
in relation to that which is not. In their complementary
ways they bear witness to the absolute otherness of God.

The God who appears and re-appears in Powys's late
stories, however, is himself a fiction, God as invented by
man: in 'Abertackle' the Devil himself declares as much. In
You and Me Um and Mo like to pretend they are God and the
Devil; and the metaphysical events and discussions are,
what they must inevitably be, aspects of play. So the
child's-eye-view and the childish style of these tales are a
mask for scepticism. They can also be disconcerting, in their
use of out-dated slang, of juvenile directness about sex and
defecation, and in Powys's cavalier disregard for scientific
propriety. But to accept the ludic nature of his material is
essential to any understanding of his handling of it.

In certain respects these stories are easier to read than their
predecesors because the element of farce, of contented wil-

fulness, is stronger. 'Topsy-Turvy' in particular takes us into Powys's private world, inhabited by such favourite boyhood authors as Harrison Ainsworth and Rider Haggard, along with the actor Henry Irving, one of the heroes of his youth and a decisive influence upon him as a lecturer. We even find a reference to his brother Theodore's garden hide-out, Bushes Home. And one notes the omnipresence of classical mythology, the familiar furniture of a mind educated in the nineteenth century.

To read these stories is to share the solitude of genius at play in extreme old age, when the fact of death is so familiar as almost to be neighbourly. The Nothing, the Void, the abysses of space which Powys evokes formed a reality that encompassed him, not as an intellectual concept but as an existential one. As Ve Zed remarks in 'Cataclysm', 'there's something in me that seems to say, fly on, fly on, fly on, fly on, and let happen what will happen.' John Cowper Powys's death was tranquil, and apparently caused by no particular disease; he simply ceased to be and thus, in the words of Jack Coffiny, his final spokesman, 'made his escape into the divine nothingness of death'.

GLEN CAVALIERO